I0641969

Joseph Needell

Passing the love of women

A Novel. Vol. 3

Joseph Needell

Passing the love of women
A Novel. Vol. 3

ISBN/EAN: 9783337273705

Printed in Europe, USA, Canada, Australia, Japan

Cover: Foto ©Andreas Hilbeck / pixelio.de

More available books at **www.hansebooks.com**

PASSING THE LOVE OF WOMEN.

A Novel.

BY

MRS. J. H. NEEDELL,

AUTHOR OF

'STEPHEN ELLICOTT'S DAUGHTER,' 'THE STORY OF PHILIP METHUEN, ETC.

IN THREE VOLUMES.
VOL. III.

LONDON:
FREDERICK WARNE AND CO.
AND NEW YORK.
1892.

[All rights reserved.]

CONTENTS OF VOL. III.

PART II. (*continued*).

PASSING THE LOVE OF WOMEN.

CHAPTER XIV.

MOTHER AND SON.

A WEEK after the accident Gilbert Yorke came to see his cousin. Mrs. Cartwright announced the visitor to her son, and suggested in the same breath that he had better not risk an interview, but content himself with sending a message of excuse.

'But, my dear mother, I have no excuse for denying myself. I am all but well, and it will give me the greatest pleasure to see him.'

'I did not suppose you would hear reason,

John,' her smile softening her words; 'but you and Gilbert Yorke never meet, I observe, without its disturbing your ordinary frame of mind, and I naturally wish to keep you from any excitement just now.'

'The disturbance does me good, mother; the ordinary flow is too sluggish.'

She looked at him with great tenderness.

'I thank God,' she said, 'that fire and quick-silver do not run in your veins as in his, or I should have played my mother's part even worse than I have.' And she went out to send the guest upstairs without giving him the chance of reply.

A minute later Gilbert knocked and entered.

John occupied his own bedroom, which, with the exception of a writing-table and a commodious bookcase, was almost as bare as in the days of his boyhood. The couch on which he lay had been brought up from the dining-room for his use, and a large rug was spread before the hearth and gave an unfamiliar air of comfort to the room. As the

August day was chilly, a good fire burnt cheerily in the capacious grate.

Even Mrs. Cartwright would have commended the quietness with which Gilbert went up to his friend. He did not speak till John's firm hand-clasp and cordial voice convinced him that he was not so ill as he had feared. Then he said, looking round:

'It is like old times, Jack, with a difference. How much better this is than the top room of the Ambassador's house in the Land Strasse! Make room on the couch for me—I want to understand how this happened.'

John asked how he had heard of the accident.

'I heard of it this morning. Did you suppose I had known it sooner? And I heard of it through Margery Denison.'

It was to the credit of John's firmness that he neither stirred nor changed colour, though his heart seemed to leap within him.

'I have her letter in my pocket,' continued

Gilbert, 'and you shall hear for yourself what she says.'

He pulled out the letter from the breast-pocket of his coat, their contiguity being such that John could see as well as if he had held it in his own hand. There was a slight indefinable perfume hanging about it, otherwise it had no distinctly feminine daintiness, the envelope being large and square and the handwriting firm and decisive.

It ran thus :

'DEAR GILBERT,

'It has just occurred to me as possible that you may not have heard of your friend Mr. Cartwright's accident, in the seclusion you choose to keep at Rookhurst. He has been knocked down by a steam-tram and severely hurt through putting his own life in jeopardy to save that of a girl who had heedlessly run into danger. I witnessed the incident, and am very anxious for authentic news of him. I should have inquired in person, but my poor father is worse than usual, and will not allow me to leave him, though, Heaven knows, I can do him no good except by the affliction of my own soul.

'Your Aunt Yorke has lent Philippa to us for a time, and we find her an immense comfort—even my father likes her.

If you are kind you will come to The Chace as soon as possible to pay your respects to one cousin and to bring us news of the other.

> 'Your affectionate friend,
>> 'MARGERY DENISON.'

John devoured the words with his eyes, while at the same time his ears hung upon the reader's voice. One sense was not sufficient, nor two even; he would like to have added a third and handled the letter, but rigorously forbore. He was conscious of a sensation of physical faintness as he watched Gilbert carefully refold the letter and restore it to his pocket.

At first he had felt a throb of exultation at the idea of there being a secret between him and Margery; that she had chosen to establish this bond of union. Then it assumed another aspect, and looked like distance and reserve; he experienced a deep satisfaction that he had kept his own counsel in the matter.

'Tell me about it, Jack,' repeated Gilbert; 'it

was scarcely the act of a friend to let me find it out in this fashion.'

'I ought to have written, or, rather, I could not write, as I have sprained the fingers of my right hand, and I thought a letter from my mother would have made too much of what is a trifle, after all.'

John spoke with solicitous kindness, because for almost the first time in his life the presence of his friend was irksome, and he would have escaped from it if he could.

Gilbert looked at him steadily.

'Is there anything wrong between us?' he asked.

'No, no,' cried the other, with an eagerness so unusual as to confirm the misgiving excited. 'Simply, I am out of tune—confinement does not agree with me.'

Gilbert smiled a little doubtfully, and, getting up from the sofa, began to walk about the room, prying into the corners and taking note of any additions or alterations that had been made, but it was only as a momentary relief from deep-seated unrest. Then he began to question John about the accident: Had he got the best advice? Was he sure there were no internal injuries? and so forth. He was to tell him all about it.

John did so in an inclusive, cursory manner, especially in regard to the 'girl' he was reported to have 'saved,' his great fear being that Gilbert would ask 'who she was' or 'if he knew her,' but his integrity was spared the dilemma.

'And you can walk about, old fellow?'

'Almost as well as ever—I am to go downstairs to-morrow. And now tell me what is on your mind. I have nothing in the world to do but to think how to help you.'

Gilbert came back to the fireplace and leaned against the mantel with his eyes on the floor.

'You read me like a book, Jack! It is a disgrace for a man to wear his heart on his sleeve as I do— only, with you, I let myself go. I am a selfish brute to bring my troubles to you when you are sick and suffering, but yet—misery like mine has its excuses.'

John Cartwright smiled slightly. He had seen a good deal of misery in the course of his short experience of life, that is, misery in the raw, as it were —overwhelming, brutalizing, not to be escaped— and the contrast between such and the speaker, so generously endowed by nature and fortune, struck him with a sort of pathetic humour.

Instantly his heart reproached him, and his understanding, too. Of what account were externals if the one boon were denied which made for happiness?

Gilbert went on : 'It is the old story—I have spoken, and she will not hear ! Were I convinced that she did not care for me, I would take my dismissal like a man, and bear it as I best could. But '—he looked up wistfully—'I think she does, and says me nay because I should lose a fortune for her dear sake.'

'But you have told her how lightly you would let that go?'

'Ay!' returned Gilbert, with the sudden vigour of the North-Country accent. 'But her way is to talk of it as a *sacrifice*—one that I should regret when it was made, and that shall not be made on her account. She is so much my friend that she takes my life into her keeping, and tears out the heart of it—then gives me back the miserable remnant, and bids me be happy!'

He turned, and began to walk up and down the room.

'You have nothing to say?' he asked presently, in a tone that bore witness to the intense irritation of his mind, for John had kept a miserable silence.

'What can I say? I—I know nothing of the way in which ladies like Miss Denison feel and reason about these things. She may possibly be influenced by a noble consideration for your cousin, Miss Yorke.'

'But I shall marry Philippa none the more because Margery refuses to marry me,' cried Gilbert eagerly. 'Though it is a shame to speak of her in this way !'

'Perhaps Miss Denison does not believe this ; she may think if you were convinced of her resolution you would hardly forego so much for so little.'

'Jack, you surprise me ! I should forego my liberty and bind myself to a horrible slavery—that of marriage with a girl I do not love, but who deserves to be loved. You, at least, will scarcely think me morally bound to marry my cousin because my grandfather has been cruel enough to make my inheritance depend upon my doing so ?'

'And hers also,' John suggested gently.

'Ah, that staggers me a little ! Sir Owen wished to bind me hand and foot, but—I refuse to be bound ! Philippa must take her modest fortune as I shall do, and please herself.'

He paused, and took a few more impatient turns through the room, very much to the distress of

John's nerves, which were greatly exercised by the pain and difficulty of the discussion. Presently he resumed speech in a tone of intense bitterness.

' I have never deceived myself by thinking much of myself—there is nothing great or heroic about me. The only power God gave me was the power of loving passionately and faithfully. He knows how I adored my mother, and how her death left me scarcely half alive; indeed, I honestly think it was only my love for Margery Denison and the hope that soon came with it—and your kindness, Jack—that kept me alive. I cannot do without her! I have not the courage to go through life under this torment of unsatisfied desire for what is noblest and best—for what I adore. Help me, Jack !'

' How is it possible for me to help you ? I would help you if I could.'

Gilbert came towards his friend, who was now sitting in a corner of the couch, and, putting his hands on his shoulders, bent over him in an attitude of urgent entreaty.

'Jack, if my life were at stake you would not need me to teach you how to plead for me. Do what you can ! She tells me again and again that she loves me dearly as—as comrade and friend. I want nothing more — I — you will understand ! There will be no indelicacy. She knows we have but one heart between us. She regards what I say as mere lover's oaths — your words will carry weight—she has the highest opinion of your judgment——'

'The thing is impossible !' said John, shrinking a little. 'It would be impossible on your own account—you will see that on reflection—a man could not stoop so low ! And on hers—it would be an intolerable impertinence—an outrage, even.'

'In that case, let it pass;' and Gilbert turned away abruptly as he spoke. 'I beg your pardon for suggesting anything that you can view in such a light, but we are poor judges of fitness when begging for dear life! Were the case reversed, I can imagine myself speaking of you in a way that need not degrade any man, and that no woman, however proud or tenacious, could resent as an outrage.'

'Ah, but I have not your facilities —your advantages!' John spoke almost with a groan.

'Forget it, Jack! What a beast selfishness makes of one! Dear old fellow, have I hurt you so much?'

He looked round the room for stimulant or cordial, but saw nothing; at the same moment there was a short, imperious knock at the door, and Mrs. Cartwright entered the room bearing in her hand an old-fashioned broth-basin, which would be exalted on shelf or cabinet to-day, containing a preparation of beef-tea to which Liebig himself might have awarded a certificate of merit.

She glanced sharply from one young man to the other, though John did his best to look composed and indifferent, and as his face was not of a flexible type, might have succeeded under less searching scrutiny.

'It is as I feared,' she said, putting down the basin, because she felt that her hand shook. 'You two, I think, never met yet but mischief was brewed between you.'

Then without warning she put her fingers on her son's wrist and was startled at the record. Unfortunately, the utmost resolution does not suffice to control our pulse-beats.

'What has happened?' she asked sternly.

'Just what you suppose,' answered Gilbert, meeting her angry glance boldly, though it needed courage; 'mischief *has* been brewed, but Jack, as usual, has had no hand in the decoction! It is all my doing. I found him so much better than I expected that I could not rest till I had poured all my troubles into his bosom. It is the old trick.'

It often annoyed Mrs. Cartwright to find that even she was not altogether proof against the winning charm of Gilbert Yorke's manner: his looks and words appeased her a little in spite of herself.

'I had scarcely thought,' she said grimly, 'that the heir of Sir Owen Yorke had any troubles to pour forth, or that my son's sympathy would have been so keen for mere fancies and conceits. But ' —more gently—'no doubt his weakness has served to strengthen it.'

'Just so,' said John eagerly. 'Gilbert was talking about a matter in which he is deeply interested—one quite remote from any concern of mine; *quite remote*—but it grieves me greatly because it grieves him. There is no secret in it, mother—we were discussing his grandfather's will.'

'Then we will hope Gilbert will postpone the subject until you are yourself again, for which reason it will be desirable for him to postpone his visits, since it is now, as ever, impossible to trust his discretion.'

She spoke in a hard, cold tone, and Gilbert felt

himself condemned and dismissed as he had done as a boy, and went away.

When he was gone Mrs. Cartwright continued to stand silently by the table where she had deposited the basin, but instead of giving it to her son she stirred the contents abstractedly and with a hand that shook with agitation.

'John,' she said after awhile, and with a flush upon her cheek that showed how deep her inward perturbation was, 'there is a question I never thought to ask my son again—have you told me a lie ?'

For a moment he was silent and a throb of indignation smote him, but when he looked at her his feeling changed.

'No,' he said, getting up and coming to her side. He hesitated a little, for she offered no encouragement; but in spite of it he put his hand, that still shook a little—for he had been profoundly moved —on her shoulder : 'I have spoken the absolute truth, believe me.'

He paused, wanting to say more — to find some outlet for the intolerable yearning of heart that had conquered him, but he could not find words. He feared, too, to betray himself—and to be misunderstood.

In the depths of the mother's heart there was an intense response to the feeling that she read in her son's eyes. But she was so fast bound in the fetters of a lifetime, that expansion and natural self-disclosure seemed as impossible to her as for the lame to walk.

She withdrew herself gently from John's hand, and said, in the quiet, measured voice which had so often closed his opening heart against her :

'I believe you implicitly in the letter, but not in the spirit, of your assurance. I should be strangely blind if I did not perceive that I am not judged worthy of your full confidence. It is a deprivation I have suffered all your life; no, we will not discuss the subject—it would do no good.'

She turned sharply and left the room, afraid of what would have been the salvation of each— lest her weakness should betray the pain and passion of her heart.

CHAPTER XV.

AN UNWELCOME DISCLOSURE.

It was not without some hesitation that Mrs. Yorke had accepted the invitation to The Chace for her daughter. She was by no means deficient in right feeling or a proper sense of womanly dignity, and she bitterly resented the fact that Gilbert had not come to see them since his return from Vienna. It was only a matter of decency that he should have communicated with her in one sense or another in respect to his intentions under his grandfather's will.

The young man was equally aware of his duty, but postponed it as one impossible to discharge, cherishing the hope that Margery Denison might yet put it in his power to make his obligations easier.

If he could go to his aunt with the statement that he was engaged to the girl he had loved from a boy, and for whom he was prepared to sacrifice his heirship, his course would be comparatively plain sailing; but so far, as we know, there seemed little chance of such help being given him. According, perhaps, to the strength and purity of a man's love is the difficulty of believing that it is powerless to kindle the heart of the woman beloved, and the very directness and simplicity of Gilbert's character seemed to hinder his comprehension of the more subtle individuality of Margery.

He went to The Chace on the following morning, because, painful as was the idea of meeting his cousin, he could not see his way to neglect Margery's summons, nor could he endure to lose the chance of seeing Margery herself; but he went with the resolution fully formed that, since he had been thus constrained to meet his cousin Philippa,

he should tell her the truth, namely, that, before
he had known even of her existence, he had given
his boyish heart to another girl, and that manhood
had confirmed the pledge.

It was, he said to himself, the only honourable
thing to do.

Gilbert was relieved to find himself shown into
an empty room, the retreating servant murmuring
something about letting Mrs. Sutherland know
that he had arrived, but he was kept waiting so
long that he began to think she had forgotten her
duty, and to wonder in what way he should make
his presence known. He hesitated to ring the bell,
knowing the state of Mr. Denison's health and
temper, lest the summons might lead to inquiry
and annoyance.

There was a piece of embroidery, with the needle
sticking in the silk, on a little table in one corner
of the deep recess formed by the bay-window,
which he took up and examined with the critical
faculty he had acquired from his mother; and he

was still holding it in his hand when at last he heard the door open and turned round to face Margery herself.

'Forgive me,' she said, advancing towards him with outstretched hand and that free grace of movement which was one of her most delightful characteristics, 'for having kept you waiting so long. I wished to see you before anyone else saw you, and my time is not now at my own disposal.'

He had never seen her look so pale and tired before, and had never felt the spell of her beauty more strongly. The weariness and pallor that would have marred another woman's face served only to add pathos to the potency of hers. She wore a white woollen wrapper, and her magnificent hair had been carelessly brushed back from the forehead and loosely plaited in one massive braid behind. The mode, adopted for the convenience of the sick-room, accentuated the perfect lines of the brow and gave a bewitching youthfulness to her appearance.

' I see—you have been up all night. Mr. Denison is worse?' he asked, and his voice was so finely tuned to the expression of the most intimate sympathy that Margery, already overwrought, turned aside so that he might not see how much it had moved her.

' Yes, but that is nothing. I could sit up for a week and thrive upon it, but it is the sight of his sufferings, his mood of mind, which disable me.' She checked a shudder and looked at him with a smile. 'How is the other invalid—Mr. Cartwright?'

Gilbert satisfied her on this point. ' All's well that ends well,' he added; ' but we should all have found it hard to forgive that woman if my cousin's life, or even his limbs, had been sacrificed to her heedlessness.'

' Ah, that is very true! You do not know, of course, who " that woman " was?'

' I do not think John knows himself,' said Gilbert a little indifferently. ' He goes about the world putting his ease and comfort, and, as it seems, even life itself, at the service of those who need them, without any respect to persons.'

Margery smiled.

'And you cannot have known him so long without catching the same spirit. I saw that you had Philippa's work in your hand as I entered. Own that it is beautifully done.'

'It is not amiss,' he returned coldly, 'but you forget in what school I have been taught.'

She looked at him wistfully, with eyes that seemed to have a new expression of gentleness and pathos. He turned away his own, lest the feelings she excited should break down his self-control, and he did not wish to take an unmanly advantage of her present mood of excited sensibility.

'If you wish to speak to me again about Philippa,' he said, 'I will listen as I have done before. But my answer will be the same. Is it worth while to waste your strength on a foregone conclusion? You have no strength to waste,' he went on anxiously. 'Sit down in this comfortable

chair and dismiss these anxieties for a little while
—you have no pity on yourself.'

' It is not that. My strength is equal to any
demands, but I have never seen death, and we are
living under its shadow. In this case it is awful !
There are no hopes beyond—not any desires, even
—and, I may say this to you, no consolations of
a well-spent life to fall back upon. In this lurid
light I see things differently. Even if one believed,
as my poor father professes to believe, that we
perish utterly like the beasts of the field, it is
horrible to leave the world no better than we found
it—to become extinct without the record of one
unselfish action !'

' All this is true,' returned Gilbert, ' but do not
dwell upon it too much. Let us comfort ourselves
with the hope that our human vision is limited,
and that on the other side blinded or baffled souls
are granted some new chance of redemption. You
make me feel afraid to speak on any other subject
when I see you like this.'

'It would be strange if you saw me otherwise, but it is in order to speak on other subjects that I am come.   Say whatever is on your mind, Gilbert.'

'I would ask, then, if in these hours of reflection you have thought of me more kindly,' he said.

'I have thought of you constantly,' was her answer, 'and have examined the case as it stands between us—and another—with as strict a desire to do right as I am capable of.   If it were a question of personal sacrifice only — supposing you would accept such a thing — I might persuade myself to become your wife and to try to do a wife's duty without a wife's love.   Forgive me if I speak with cruel frankness; you will own it is better to be plain.'

She stopped a moment, then went on again :

'Don't you see that I should sacrifice not only myself, but you?   You would either openly rebel against the limitations of my feelings or secretly resent them—either way, it would end in alienation and misery. Under these circumstances it would be impossible for you to forget that you gave the go-by to a splendid inheritance and all the enormous privileges that belong to it, and that you had been cheated in the equivalent. No, do not interrupt me. I have not done.'

'Only one word! The argument would be convincing were it not based on a false assumption. Once my wife—God help me, the words set my brain on fire!—you should love me to the height of your capacity and my desire. What then?'

'Ah, there is nothing left,' cried Margery, with a sudden burst of impetuosity, 'but to tell you the truth! There is one difficulty that no man, however generous or devoted, can overcome; I—I am not free to be conquered by your love, or I think I must have yielded——'

She stopped, the warm pallor of face and neck suffused with a deep flush that passed and left her paler than before, and her eyes, full of a proud shame, downcast before his riveted gaze. Then with a suppressed groan he looked away from her.

'I need not ask if this is true,' was his answer; 'I see that it is true.'

He began to walk about the room, wrestling with the sense of hopeless defeat brought home to him at last. The desire to know who this other man was—crowned with a blessedness above his possible deserts—was a consuming one; but it would have run against the fine grain of his nature to have questioned her, however indirectly.

His forbearance, his acceptance and his evident distress touched Margery profoundly. She spoke again in a low, troubled voice:

'I want you to understand why I have told you this. It is because it would have been a crime to stand by silent and see two lives sacrificed in vain. Is it worth while now to give up everything—for so little?'

'Everything?' he repeated bitterly. 'You have left me nothing!'

He stopped, then began again :

'I have not even the right to complain. You see, I have always hoped against hope that I should win you in the end, and the blindness of it all—the folly—the madness stings me with shame and a sort of remorse. What a fool you must have thought me ! And yet, why did you not tell me sooner ?'

'I think,' she answered in the lowest of tones and with her hand shading her face, ' I think I have told you almost as soon as I knew myself. The truth has only come to me lately—by my poor father's bedside. I told you I had learnt many things there—I have learnt this.'

He looked at her intently, knowing that her own eyes were hidden. She had never appeared to him so sweet and womanly, or so infinitely to be desired, as at this moment when he realized that she was lost to him for ever.

'There is one question——' he began, but she interrupted him with a little gesture of deprecation.

'Do not be afraid,' he resumed. 'The question

I am going to ask is not one that you need refuse
to answer.   Is this man worthy?'

'Worthy, you mean, of honour and love?   Yes,
he is worthy.'

It was on his lips to question her further, but he
forbore.

'I will go away,' he said, 'lest I should be tempted
to say anything that might hurt or vex you.   That
is as much as I can do—it is not in me to wish you
happiness—elsewhere.   Mine has been cut down
at the root, and I can feel nothing now but the
insufferable smart.   You have never understood,
Margery, how I have loved you.'

'I know, I know,' she said humbly.   'It would
have been hard to have done you justice.   I almost
hate myself that I have not been able to give you
what you wanted.'

He had turned to depart, when a sudden thought
struck him.

'Was it this,' he asked sharply, 'that you wished
to say "before I saw anyone else"?   Was it the

better to fit me for paying my respects to my cousin?'

'No,' she said, rousing herself to her task with some effort, for she was tired and exhausted. 'I never meant to let my secret escape me; my mind was full of other thoughts. Even now I must entreat you to stay while I try to make you understand what it is that I want. Do not go!'

She hesitated, fearing to lose her object through maladroitness or persistency, and yet painfully aware that the present opportunity was probably the last that would be given her. A look of hardness, too, had come into Gilbert's face that discouraged her.

'Why,' he asked, 'should you take the trouble to explain your purpose, when at any rate it is frustrated? I shall see no one else under your roof —perhaps not at any time—certainly not to-day. With your leave, Margery, I will go.'

'You must not go,' she pleaded, 'before you have seen your cousin Philippa. Understand that she knows that you are in the house and will take it very unkindly; and you must know even better than I how tender and sensitive she is.'

'It will be necessary,' he answered, with a sternness quite new to him, 'that my cousin Philippa should learn to expect nothing from me.'

'You mean that you are still resolutely bent on disinheriting yourself—and her? It may seem so at this moment, but other thoughts will come—wiser and more kind. Gilbert, have we ceased to be friends? Will you not grant one consolation to the woman for whom you have been willing to forego—I will say nothing of fortune—but, as you have told her, even life itself?'

His eyes flashed.

'You are taking an unfair advantage of our position! For the woman to make requests at the very moment that she has robbed me of the hope that was more even than the life I offered her, is not only ungenerous, but cruel! Yes, Margery, we have ceased to be friends—I could not bear it.'

'Then you leave me miserable beyond my power
to express! I shall wish that I had never crossed
your path, though in that case I should have missed
the chief of the sunshine that has fallen on mine!
Go, if you will, in this spirit; but before you go,
ask yourself if it is not as hard for me to have
the friendship which has been the pride and joy
of my life thrown contemptuously behind your
back as for you to be refused—what I cannot
give?'

This touched him.

'I do not know,' he said restlessly. 'I am not
able to weigh the imponderable nor to argue about
spirit and flame as you do! But'—looking at her
as if afraid to trust himself—'what task did you
want to set me?'

'Such a task as a temper like yours will find
it impossible on reflection to refuse. I want to
engage you not to bar my own way to a possible
happiness nor to break your cousin's heart. Understand, I do not speak in figures. Philippa explains

your avoidance of her by dislike and contempt, and the pain and shame of it are killing her.'

'I will undeceive her on that point,' he said gently, 'though not to-day. I will tell her the simple truth, and she will hold me justified.'

'You will kill her all the same, for her life is so frail it will never bear the shock of that disclosure. Do not make any mistake in this matter. It is become a question of right or wrong, not of mere choice or rejection. Circumstances, however hard they may be, have made you responsible not only for the happiness of this girl, but for her very existence, and you will be guilty of a crime if you refuse, out of consideration for yourself, to fulfil your duty towards her. No, I will not admit your disclaimers. You are free and able to do this thing. I feel all the ungraciousness of these words from my mouth, but I dare not go back to my father and leave them unspoken.'

'And you can seriously propose to me as a duty to hoodwink my cousin, to lie to her against my own heart and conscience, and to marry her under false pretences! The point you have forgotten to take into account is what will happen when her awakening comes.'

' Oh, but there is to be no such dishonesty and no deceit!' cried Margery with indignant energy. ' I would not have Philippa cheated by a hair's breadth. Is it not possible for you to reassure her mind to-day by showing her just the same kindness you have always shown her? Keep the secret of our relations until she is grown stronger in health and confident in your affection ; it will not hurt her sweet humility to take the second place in your regard, and as to the " awakening," that must be to a better and nobler life—aye, and love, too—than you and I should ever reach together.'

He shook his head. ' I cannot do it—it is beyond me! Years hence perhaps, when I have grown callous, if that time ever comes—only then it will be too late for your purpose. Margery, you have hit upon a refinement of cruelty. For you to plead for Philippa hardens my heart against her.'

'I know! I know! But what can I do? I have seen her every hour of the day, and I can read her heart. Dear, it is just this; you cannot have what is wanted, but you can give just this to another, and in so doing will heal your own wound. Do not laugh at hearing Margery Denison preaching magnanimity; it will come easy to you, for you have it by inheritance.'

'No, I never had that! I can only be good to those I love—to none others. I should be a bad husband to Philippa, and should break her heart only a little later. But, then, I should have secured Rookhurst!' He spoke with intense bitterness.

Margery sighed, it must be owned a little impatiently.

'I must go back to my father,' she said, 'or he will be asking for me, but I cannot go back beaten at all points. Give me a little comfort to take with me. Promise me this small thing if you refuse the greater—be kind to Philippa, explain your neglect by your illness or as you will, and, if you will give no pledges, at least enter into no dis- closures for a month or two. Is this too much for you to grant?'

'It is too much for you to ask,' was his answer, 'but I yield as I would yield a limb, or my life, to serve you! Only I cannot visit Philippa under your roof.'

'That is already arranged. She goes home next week. I would not keep her here in the present depressing influences. But—you will consent to see her to-day? Dear, do not think me heartless. She is watching and waiting and listen- ing for her summons. I told her this visit was for her. If you leave the house without seeing her it will be useless to follow her to Fair Lawns. But I see—I need say no more. God bless you, dear, dearest of friends.'

Her face was flushed with a noble ardour, and she held out both her hands to him. Gilbert grasped them hard, and looked at her with despairing eyes from which hope and appeal were vanished. It seemed to draw her heart towards him with the yearning protective affection he had always inspired, and as a sudden reminiscence flashed across her mind she leaned towards him, and would have touched his forehead with her lips, but he drew back sharply.

'Not that,' he said; 'I could not bear it.'

He dropped her hands and turned away to the window, nor did he look round till he had heard the door open and shut, and knew that he was alone.

CHAPTER XVI.

A few days later John Cartwright was sitting at his writing-table in his bedroom, which now served the purpose of his study, preparing his Sunday's sermon, when a servant knocked at the door to say that a lady had called and wished to see him.

The circumstance was not an unusual one. The social and religious organizations in connection with Castle Street Chapel were in a high state of activity, and the young minister was the favourite referee of the workers in his flock in any case of difficulty, or, indeed, as he was sometimes inclined to think, where no difficulty existed.

John rose with a sigh; he was just warming to

his work, and the interruption was unwelcome. He knew that the probability was he would be confronted with some Sunday-school teacher or missionary collector whose business might have been better discussed at the weekly class-meeting.

'You are quite sure that the lady asked for me, and not for my mother?' he said, with an instinctive struggle towards self-preservation.

The maid was quite sure; besides, the mistress was out; and then she added:

'The lady is Miss Denison, of The Chace.'

John stooped over his books. 'Say I will be with her directly.'

He sat for full five minutes with his face in his hands, waiting till his power of will had reduced the fierce beatings of his heart and given him back his self-control. It was perhaps this exercise of mastery that gave an unfamiliar air of dignity to his manner and seemed to obliterate his usual social awkwardness when he entered the room.

Margery was sitting in his mother's chair, slowly

swaying herself to and fro. The vision thus presented had an element of household allurement in it that worked like a gratuitous test of his endurance. Her attire always seemed to him to possess a sort of imperial elegance, but his experience on such points was limited, and Margery was one of those women who do not so much borrow effects from their clothes as bestow them. But his next glance showed him that she was looking pale and weary.

'I am sorry,' he said, slightly touching the hand she had extended as she rose to meet him, 'that my mother is not at home, since you have done her the honour to call.'

There was so great a restraint in his manner as to produce in the mind of the girl he addressed a chill sense of alarm, until reflection suggested the obvious and encouraging explanation. She smiled a little faintly, for her spirits were greatly depressed and her energy at a low ebb.

'I should have been glad to have seen Mrs.

Cartwright, but my business is with you. I will explain it at once, lest we might be interrupted. My father, as perhaps you know, is very ill. I mean that the end is not far off, and his state of mind is that of blank utter unbelief. This makes his sister, my dear aunt, so miserable that she has tried again and again to argue with him—with the very worst results. He will not allow her now to enter his room. In this emergency she has sent me to you. She thinks that perhaps you would see him.'

'Would Mr. Denison consent to see me?'

'I do not know. We thought it best to get your promise to come before we suggested the idea. Will you come if I am so happy as to be able to send you a message?'

John stood thinking profoundly, with his eyes on the ground.

'If you send for me I will come,' he said, looking up, 'because no sense of unworthiness can excuse a man from the attempt to do his duty.

But this seems to me a sort of spiritual forlorn hope, and I would urgently beg that someone better qualified by age and standing—someone more acceptable, naturally, than I can be to Mr. Denison, should be chosen.'

' My poor father has long alienated the clergy of Copplestone, if your words point to them, Mr. Cartwright. There is not one with whom he has not some quarrel, more or less personal, or that he would consent to admit to his bedside. It is because of your youth, and the absence of all clerical assumption on your part, that my aunt hopes for a better reception.'

She waited, but as he still continued silent she repeated her question :

' If we send for you may we depend on your coming ?'

' I cannot refuse to do so, though I confess I would escape the ordeal if I dared. I shall come, Miss Denison,' he continued with his grave smile, ' like the shepherd-boy of the East, with my sling and few pebbles from the brook; but it will be to contend against a more formidable antagonist, and my faith is too feeble to hope for victory.'

'And yet I should have thought from your sermons and—from what I hear of you—that your belief was so firmly established as to enable you to give a conclusive answer to all objections and cavillings, however erudite.'

He smiled. 'Then you are very much mistaken. There is not a single branch of knowledge or human experience concerning which a child, much more a man of Mr. Denison's calibre, may not be able to perplex a philosopher, and in regard to belief or disbelief in the Christian religion I do not suppose any sceptic ever yet was converted by argument. We leave aside the impossibility of dispassionate discussion with a dying man.'

Margery opened wide her beautiful eyes.

'Pardon me, but in that case what inducement have you to try?'

'I should not presume to try to argue about the

evidences of our faith, because I do not believe that the mere external testimony of history will ever produce conviction until the man has already been made responsive to the idea of his need of redemption. I think this sense of need is inherent in human nature, be that nature what it may, and however strenuously it may be denied or stamped out. It is the final verdict of experience that faith in Christ is the outcome, not of the intellect, but of that spiritual apprehensiveness which is as absolute and authoritative as reason itself.'

'I think,' said Margery in a tone of intense feeling, 'that to be redeemed from himself is the most passionate desire of my poor father's soul, though, no doubt, he would rather die than confess it. But I own, Mr. Cartwright, even if one accepts your theory, that it seems to me quite as hard to produce this responsive attitude of mind as intellectual conviction itself.'

John hesitated and coloured. 'I feel painfully,'

was his answer, ' how the deep things of religion suffer through the perils of human expression. But we work under the inspiration of One whose strength fortifies our weakness. Do you think I would dare to face Mr. Denison otherwise? I am very much afraid of him.'

' Did you ever speak to him ?' she asked in some surprise.

' Never. But I once heard him speak to my cousin Gilbert, on the first occasion that I ever saw you.'

' Oh !' she cried eagerly and with a vivid blush, ' I beseech you to forget that incident! The re-collection of it covers me with shame. Believe that since those days I at least have grown in—in knowledge of the world—in independence of mind —in——'

She stopped short; an invincible confusion made the words drag on her tongue. John, too, was looking at her with an expression that she could not quite define—it seemed eloquent of feeling, but of feeling so complex and veiled that it filled her with a vague apprehension.

'I am the last to whom that assurance is necessary,' he said. 'I carry in my mind too exact a remembrance of your generous kindness on the occasion when—when we met last.'

'Have you kept our secret?' she asked, with a charming archness.

In spite of himself, he could not help smiling back into the lovely face.

'I thought that you would prefer that I should. One does not care to make public such an experience as that.'

The colour deepened in her cheek.

'You mean that even your mother does not know?'

'There seemed to me no reason that she should. I think, Miss Denison, we will agree never to refer to the subject again.'

Her eyes dwelt upon him with a secret shy pleasure. The very reserve and deference of his manner, the implications that she attached to his words, soothed and yet animated her mind. Was it likely, indeed, that this man, obscure and unattractive, whom by a sort of womanly perversity she had chosen to love, would be able to resist that influence to which so many had yielded, even amongst those whose experience was so much wider and more brilliant?

'That shall be as you please,' was her answer, 'after to-day. I have been compelled to yield to the hindrances which prevented my fulfilling my promise to call upon your mother, but I trusted your fidelity; even though appearances were against me, I knew you would not think me ungrateful.'

'You not only discharged your debt on the spot,' he said gravely, 'but reversed the obligation.'

'Ah, you set too much value on the current coin of thanks! But about yourself: are you sure you are quite recovered from the shock—that no mischief has resulted? I thought—excuse me—that you looked a little paler and thinner when you came in.'

John did not answer at once ; he was looking not at the speaker, but straight before him, as if in search of the hardihood of which he stood in need, and as he faced the garden he saw his mother approaching the house, and the next moment he heard the click of the opening gate.

His cheek, which justified Margery's remark, flushed a little, and an unspoken thanksgiving swelled his heart: his unpractised fortitude had been enduring too severe a strain.

He turned to his visitor with a brightening eye and a look of relief.

'I see my mother, Miss Denison—she is just coming in. She will be proud to make your acquaintance.'

Margery made a charming little gesture of deprecation.

'There is no escape ; but, like yourself, I have my weaknesses, and one of them is a wholesome fear of your mother. However, I will do my best.'

The best was perfect. The graceful deference of her manner disarmed Mrs. Cartwright's sensitive anxiety, which had taken ready alarm on finding her son *tête-à-tête* with so great a lady, and the object of her visit, which Margery hastened to explain, with the implied recognition of that son's spiritual worth, brought to the mother's heart the purest joy of which it was susceptible.

The sweetness of the girl's courtesy was contagious. John watched his mother with a grateful surprise. She spoke of Mr. Denison with a chastened sympathy that he could scarcely have supposed possible, and offered the hospitality of their early dinner as an equivalent for luncheon with a cordiality so winning that Margery was sorely tempted to avail herself of it.

'I should like so much to stay,' she said, 'but I dare not. I have been absent from home some time now, and my father will miss me. I am so happy as to feel at last that I am of some use to him.'

'At last!' repeated Mrs. Cartwright, looking at her with a smile that pleased Margery better than the most elaborate of compliments, and then she added, with a consideration for which her son blessed her :

'But, my dear young lady, you must not let your zeal outrun your discretion. I am an old nurse myself, and can read pretty well the story of your pale cheeks and tired eyes. Sick people grow selfish, unless they are saints indeed, and it is the truest kindness to deny them in order to serve them better.'

Margery rose to go, explaining that she had left her carriage in the town at the Stukely Arms, in order that their old coachman, in whom her aunt had much greater confidence than in herself, might fulfil certain commissions.

'Then you will allow John to walk down with you and see you in safe keeping ?'

LIBRARY

There was obviously no alternative, and the walk formed an era in the young man's life; he had never but once walked by the side of a beautiful woman before, and this woman he secretly adored, so that the present rapture held despair at bay. Then she talked to him delightfully—not of himself, for that was torture—but of his mother, praising and admiring with a gracious sincerity and discrimination which were sweet to his ears. When she again fell back on the subject of her father, he discovered in all she said a nobleness and self-devotion for which he had always given her credit in common with all other gifts and graces, but which at the same time it was the greatest comfort to him to see manifested beyond all controversy.

Her last words were, as she seated herself in the carriage :

'Hold yourself in readiness for my summons— it will surely come !

CHAPTER XVII.

JOHN CARTWRIGHT did receive his summons to The Chace, but it was to advise and console Mrs. Sutherland under the deep distress of mind she experienced at the sudden and unexpected termination of her brother's long illness. Cyril Denison died on the evening of the day of Margery's visit to Elm Lodge.

He had been slowly wearing towards death for the last ten years, and more actively dying for as many months, and yet when the end came it came as a surprise; but it is the experience of humanity that, however watched and waited for, the King of Terrors always comes upon us unawares.

Mrs. Sutherland, weak and emotional, and long tried by her brother's tyranny, had lately turned for solace to the excitements and consolations of religion as presented by the double pastorate of Castle Street Chapel, and her first impulse ' when all was over ' was to send for John Cartwright and discuss with him the agonizing probabilities of her brother's future state.

Margery, who was present at the interview, but scarcely spoke, received a deep impression of his patience, tenderness and wisdom. The inconsequence of her aunt's mind was to herself a constant provocation, and she thought it had never appeared under a more trying form. She appealed to the young minister with a sort of querulous persistence, as if the secrets of the unknown and the unrevealed world either were or should be open to his ken, and she invested him with the power of absolute decision on the points of her pathetic anxiety.

Under the pressure of her distress, her faculties

were unusually confused, and she would repeat under another form the same inquiry to which he had already returned an answer, to find it met with the same sympathetic patience and forbearance.

When he rose at last to go away, Mrs. Sutherland begged him to return soon, assuring him what a comfort he had been to her. She confided to him all their family affairs, telling him that they had no one to undertake for them. The heir was in Africa, and they were not on good terms; her poor brother had quarrelled with the family solicitors, and she did not really know where to turn for advice; she and her niece would be leaving The Chace, perhaps the neighbourhood: 'would he allow her to look upon him in the light of a friend?'

John acquiesced. His personal desire was to avoid Margery as an element of peril and unrest in a life he was bound to keep calm and ordered, but his principle of action was to help those who claimed help.

In bidding him good-bye, Margery said :

' I am far more unhappy, Mr. Cartwright, than if my father and I had been like other fathers and daughters. There is something hopeless in the knowledge that one has missed the natural chances and joys of life.'

Her tone and manner were intensely sad and dejected, and she looked pale and worn with watching. John's own experience confirmed her words, though a feeling of loyalty held back the open expression of sympathy ; but there was a look in his eyes that told of an intimate comprehension.

' I see you understand,' she said softly, ' though it can scarcely be of your own knowledge.' Then she added : ' You will like to know ; I was with him when he died ; it was a gentle dismissal, as calm as the falling asleep of a child. I thank God there were no terrors, and, alas ! there were no last words.' Her eyes brimmed. ' Perhaps you would not believe it, but no girl has ever lived a more desolate life than I. I had no mother, and have always been—alone.'

'If the offer of any help I can render is not presumption,' was his answer, ' use it as seems good to you.'

As if to increase the difficulties of his situation, Mrs. Cartwright had received a strong impression in Margery's favour, and was eager to be of service as soon as she knew that service would be welcomed.

The circumstances of the ladies at The Chace were an open secret. Mr. Denison had died heavily in debt, and his quarrel with the heir had been so gratuitous and bitter that nothing was to be expected from his liberality.

Margery inherited the annual two hundred pounds that had been settled on her mother, so that she was spared the pain of absolute depend-ence upon her aunt, and they were both anxious to rid themselves of the responsibilities of a big house as soon as possible, and to take one more suited to their means. Travel had been suggested at first, but the plan was postponed by mutual consent. Martin Cartwright was the owner of considerable property in the neighbourhood of Copplestone, and Mrs. Sutherland had thought proper to take him into consultation about their affairs. Amongst other investments he had recently bought a pretty old-fashioned house, standing in half an acre of garden, that was quite capable of being improved into a desirable abode. It was situated on the Seamoor Road, half-way between The Chace and Copplestone, and had been offered by the wealthy draper to the two ladies on the most advantageous terms. It would take a month or two to put in thorough repair, but, then, Margery had received a kind letter from the absent heir, begging her to retain the use of The Chace as long as it suited her convenience, and assuring her that he was prepared to act at all points as a kinsman should.

The result of all this was to bring John and Margery frequently together, and to establish a recognised friendship between them, that he at least had never believed possible.

Margery brightened and sweetened under the influence, for so entire was his devotion to her service, whether it took the form of practical help in their affairs or of willingness to discuss any question in which she was interested, that she never guessed that each occasion when they met was in fact an act of renunciation.

To see her constantly under this aspect of delightful friendliness was to fan the flame of his passion, and to add to the stringency of the struggle by which he tried to keep it under control. He felt himself no more justified in refusing her behests than those of any other woman to whom it was possible for him to be useful ; but there were times, as he sat alone in his room at night, when the remembrance of the light in Margery's eyes, or of some happy phrase that had fallen from her lips, or of the recent touch of her hand, wrought upon him almost to the point of physical torture.

Once in a moment of unusual weakness he had suffered his mind to rest upon the idea of her loving him in return : not as a possibility, but as a dream, until his strong swarthy face glowed and softened into positive beauty, and for a few delicious moments he tasted that fine rapture which happy lovers know.

His deep-rooted conviction still was that Margery, while denying the fact to herself as well as to others, really loved Gilbert Yorke, and that her rejection was based partly on a curious blindness, but mainly on the generous grounds of her reluctance to rob him of his inheritance and to traverse Philippa's interests.

It is scarcely necessary to say that this notion invested Margery with that element of high-souled disinterestedness without which the young minister would have found less justification for his love, while at the same time it stood between him and any possible apprehension of the real state of her feelings.   He referred every tone and touch of

kindness—and they were many—either to the glow
and warmth of her own free nature or to the
special favour shown to him because he had the
privilege of being the chosen friend of Gilbert
Yorke.

CHAPTER XVIII.

MRS. YORKE PRESENTS THE SITUATION.

IT was greatly to the credit of Gilbert Yorke's powers of self-control and sweetness of disposition that he played his part so well in the interview with his cousin Philippa, which succeeded the painful passage between himself and Margery, that the girl never suspected how much the effort cost him.

She came into the room where he awaited her after a long interval, which he owed doubtless to the consideration of Margery, and her own embarrassment had been so painful that his first desire was to put her at her ease. He could not help talking kindly to an old friend, and especially

when that friend looked so pale and fragile as
Philippa. He knew, too, that the influence of her
home life made her morbidly shy and self-distrust-
ful, and perceived that on this occasion she seemed
in actual terror of what he might be going to say.
So by mutual consent they touched only the surface
of things, he telling her about his recent illness, in
which she seemed greatly interested, and asking
for news of her mother and brother with the affectionate, sympathetic ease which had marked their
relations from the first.

Philippa revived under this treatment; the sight
of her cousin alone was like water in the desert, for
the secret thirst to see him had long been consuming the springs of health and vigour, and the
one subject that she dreaded him to approach was
that in which their mutual fate was implicated.
She had never dared to indulge the hope of a
blessedness beyond the dreams of poetry and
romance, until she knew that if he passed her over
he passed over at the same time that which might

have made any man hesitate, and her humility was such that she would have accepted gratefully a tithe of the love that she bestowed. To sit in the light of his countenance, to hear and to serve him, would almost have satisfied her. She had always felt a painful sense of inferiority, but now, as she timidly marked the improvement in Gilbert's appearance, the increased distinction and manliness of his bearing, added to the old remembered charm, this feeling lay upon her heart like a stone.

Therefore it was with no disappointment, but with the relief of a prisoner whose sentence is deferred, that she found that her cousin met her on the same friendly footing as before, and was not alienated by the cruel restriction of their grandfather's will. He told her that he was going away for two or three weeks for change of air, but that immediately on his return he should come and see them at Fair Lawns, and he sent kind messages to his aunt and to Edward.

It was with an intense anxiety that Margery had

watched for her after Gilbert's departure, but Philippa's shining eyes and sweet smile set her heart at rest. She forbore to question her, but the girl's heart was too full not to overflow.

'He was so kind and good,' she said; 'just the same as ever. He is coming to see us as soon as he returns from abroad.'

Philippa still used the primitive expression; she herself had never stirred out of England.

'Where is he going?' asked Margery with secret anxiety.

'To Leipzig.' And then she added, with deep seriousness: 'Margery, you have known so many people—did you ever know anyone like him?'

Margery stooped, and, framing the small sweet face in her hands, kissed her on the lips and forehead.

'Never, dear! There is but one Gilbert Yorke in the world, and he was born to make you happy.'

Her conscience smote her as she spoke; it seemed like taking advantage of the man who had behaved so well at such a crisis, and she saw that Philippa's eyes brimmed and sank, and that she blushed with painful intensity.

'We will not speak of that,' said the girl. 'If he were born for me it is a very poor destiny.'

Philippa dreaded her return home, but there was no alternative under the circumstances of Mr. Denison's approaching dissolution. The close questioning she had expected from her mother, and the gibes and sneers of Edward, had to be endured; but she found them more intolerable even than she had feared. It was scarcely unreasonable that Mrs. Yorke should cherish a lively displeasure against her nephew, but her open threat that if he did not come, according to the promise that Philippa reported, she should write and demand an explanation of his intentions, threw the poor girl into an agony of apprehension.

It became one of the petitions in her daily prayers that Gilbert should keep his promise, and spare her the shame of this appeal.

But Gilbert had every intention of keeping his word. He had gone to Leipzig as to a place endeared to his memory, and with the unacknowledged feeling that if so cruel a wound as his could be soothed, the balm was more likely to be found there than anywhere else; and it must be owned that the first evening he spent amongst new pupils and old masters at the *Conservatoire* confirmed this belief.

He did more than this; for the few days which followed his interviews with Margery and with his cousin he had consented to weigh the possibility of accepting Sir Owen's will, and with it the *rôle* of a life-long sacrifice. But the constitutional concentration of his character—the personal passion he threw into every detail of life—made the idea specially obnoxious. Men of wider interests and of a less eager temper might more easily have reconciled themselves to a loveless marriage, but it represented to Gilbert Yorke the degradation of his integrity and of his manhood, and so soon as the spell of his art caught him the old ambition revived and clinched his conviction.

Surely it was enough for the woman who refused him to compass her personal happiness without dictating the terms of his own bondage; he was doing no wrong to Philippa, for no word beyond kind, cousinly feeling had ever passed his lips, nor did he believe (but here his conscience pricked him) that her regard was of a warmer character. Nor was she a girl who would deplore the loss of wealth and position; rather her desire would be to escape such a burden, and the modest fortune which his rejection would secure her was adequate to meet her simple wants.

Therefore, difficult as the task would be, he would go straight to his aunt on his return and demonstrate to her that he could not marry his cousin. He would not spare his pride, but tell her that the only woman he could ever wish to make his wife would not have him, and that in his view a life-long celibacy was the alternative.

When he reached London, after a month's absence, he deliberated as to whether he should run down to Yorkshire and take John into his confidence before going to Fair Lawns. He was aware of Mr. Denison's death, and of Mrs. Sutherland's plans, for his cousin was always a faithful correspondent, and held the boyish engagement of supplying him with all the information in his power concerning Margery Denison as still binding; the personal difficulty of doing so making the obligation rather the more than the less imperative.

But Gilbert gave up the notion. He was eager to get through what he knew would be a very unpleasant and difficult business, that would perhaps be more painful to himself than to anyone else, and he was not sure what view of his duty John Cartwright might take. He would see him when all was over and he was a free man, if a disappointed one.

He found the household at Fair Lawns under

a cloud. Fair Lawns was a pretty place, but it stood low, and the house was too closely surrounded with shrubs and trees. The river, which ran under willow banks at the bottom of the gardens, was a charming object in spring and summer, but was apt to be depressing and miasmatic in autumn. Mrs. Yorke was barely convalescent from an attack of bronchitis, which she attributed to her surroundings, and the young baronet's health and temper were both at their worst.

The aunt's reception of her nephew indicated an armed neutrality, and so irksome did Gilbert find the condition of things, that he had no resource but to devote himself to Philippa through the long evening that followed his arrival. He had suggested the piano to her, though he knew she was a poor musician, and had produced his violin, when, his own ardour being enough for him, he had played divinely some of his recent Leipzig acquisitions. The girl had no faculty of musical comprehension, but the proposal gave her full liberty to watch the performer, and served to add a little fresh fuel to the flame of her innocent love. The diversion was finally stopped by a peremptory protest from Edward's chamber.

'The sound of a fiddle,' he said, 'was one of the many things he could not endure. It tore him in two!'

On the following morning Gilbert asked for an interview with his aunt, feeling that he had never realized the extreme awkwardness of the situation until he found himself face to face with that cold and august personage. Nevertheless, he fulfilled his task of explanation as best he could, well assured from Mrs. Yorke's aspect that, however inadequate his words might have been, he had succeeded in making clear his refusal to accept the conditions of his grandfather's will.

For a few moments she sat silent; then, lifting her fine blue eyes from the ground, she looked at him steadily and said:

'It is now six months since Sir Owen's death:

will you kindly explain to me how it is that you have not made your intentions known to me before? During that period everyone has regarded my daughter in the light of your future wife, and the poor child has the same impression. You were bound as a man of honour, if it were your intention from the beginning to repudiate this will, to have communicated the fact to your lawyers and to mine without loss of time. As the case now stands——'

'You forget! I was very ill, so ill as to know nothing till long after——'

She interrupted him. 'I admit there was a delay of a few weeks, not longer. Sir Owen died in June, and you were at Rookhurst in July. Your behaviour was so extraordinary that I asked Mr. Percival what conclusion I was to draw from it, and his answer was that as the young man was a gentleman, it could be understood only in one way —that he accepted his inheritance on the terms offered. The bequest in our eyes was an act of cruel injustice. Do you propose to add to the wrong you have done the brother the still greater wrong of rejecting the sister? If so, you deliberately subvert the intentions of the testator.' She spoke without passion, in a cold, incisive tone that seemed to make the arguments with which he had fortified his decision poor and inadequate.

'I act in this way,' he answered, 'because I believe that Philippa cares as little about fortune as I do myself, and that even if she cared more she would not consent to take for her husband a man who does not love her. I feel sure she would honour my motive and would set me free. I feel for her as a brother might feel, and I think her affection for me is of the same sort. May I explain myself to her?'

'That is a matter for future consideration. If I have understood you aright, your first point of explanation will be that you are in love with somebody else. That might present more difficulty if the lady in question were in love with you, but you also tell me, with admirable candour, that she has rejected your addresses. I know not,' Mrs. Yorke added in a lower tone, 'what woman of honour would have done otherwise under the circumstances.'

These words startled Gilbert, once more raising the passionate doubt in his mind whether the last avowal by which Margery had silenced his suit might not have been prompted by some extravagance of generosity rather than by the truth.

'It is true that I have been rejected,' was his answer; 'but that does not alter the case. I shall love her till the last hour of my life, and therefore I refuse to marry elsewhere.'

'But that decision is not open to you—at least, as a man of honour. When Sir Owen signed his egregious will it was under the intention that the wrong done to Edward should be redressed to Philippa. He knew that my poor little girl, who has seen nothing of the world, was fond of you, and would be willing to be the means of enriching you.

If you refuse to fulfil the contract, it will not only
be robbing her of what her grandfather meant her
to enjoy, but will be offering her personally an
insult, that can be offered with impunity because
she has no one to defend her except a woman and
a cripple.'

'I think,' he said, shrinking, 'you might, in
justice, have spared me that.'

'I will spare you nothing of the truth, for to
keep it back would only be to lay up remorse for
you in the future. For six months I have seen my
child growing thinner and paler under the strain of
hope deferred. It is hard for a mother to confess
this, but I have no alternative. You know how
frail her health is, but she can bloom and expand
in the sunshine. Since she came back from The
Chace she has been another creature : this morning, last night, she was radiant. I believe, though
no complaint will ever pass her lips, and she will
deny her love to her last breath, that if you deal
her this blow of repudiation she will sink under it.

You will then have completed your work.' She paused with no simulated emotion, and added : ' Is it worth while to forego Rookhurst as well as break a girl's heart ?'

He made no reply, but she could see that her words were telling, and hastened to strike again while the iron was hot.

'The question narrows itself to this,' she said quietly : 'Are you going to write yourself large in the eyes of the world as something quite otherwise than a man of honour ?'

'Oh, if you knew how little I care for the world and its judgments !' he returned passionately. ' It is to myself that I justify myself ! I should cause my cousin more suffering by marrying than by leaving her, even if it be as you say. I know my own limitations. I could not feign fondness—I should be a bad husband to the wife I did not love.'

Mrs. Yorke's face flushed with anger. She rose impatiently, and then sat down again ; hitherto

she had been very temperate, but now her voice
shook with passion as she answered :

' You mean me to understand that this is your
ultimatum? You have the matchless effrontery to
come to my house and tell me, in the face of all
that I have confessed to you, that you would rather
beggar yourself and your cousin than marry her?
It is not to be borne !'

' What can I do otherwise?' asked Gilbert, in
distress. ' To whom else should I have come? It
is hard and cruel! I hate myself for what I have
been compelled to say. I am bitterly sorry, but I
see no other way.'

She looked at his pale, set face, marked the
sensitive vibrations of his voice, and felt that all
was not yet lost.

' Gilbert,' she said, ' let me speak to you as a
mother. You are in the first heat of a young man's
disappointment, and believe that it will last for ever.
Is the experience of life to count for nothing? May
I not be allowed to believe that what you now put

from you as distasteful will prove in the end your best consolation? I know the circumstances are cruel, for they do not admit of delay, but——'

Her eyes filled with tears.

'Do not urge me!' he pleaded. 'It is just because I know how sweet and good she is—how fit to be wooed and won by the best amongst us— that I will not insult her by believing that she would take me as I am. Let me go, Aunt Yorke, and forget that I ever existed.'

'That will be difficult,' she said, with intense bitterness, 'seeing that whenever I look at my son I must remember him who robbed him of his birthright and, not content with that, flung away what he had got in order to mar Philippa's life as well. I never loved my father-in-law, Sir Owen Yorke; I had little reason. But there seems something pitiful in this overthrow of all his schemes. And yet he was very good to you!'

Gilbert kept silence. It seemed as if Fate were driving him resistlessly against his will and his conscience. What Mrs. Yorke urged in one way, Margery had urged in another, and the pity of it was that there was so much to be granted on their side. He could not deny that Mrs. Yorke had valid grounds for disappointment, and that his rejection of his cousin, however justified in his own sight, did look like an act of base ingratitude to his grandfather's memory.

'I am in a grievous strait,' he said at last. 'I must go over this ground again, though I had hoped——'

He hesitated, stopped, and, looking up, met Mrs. Yorke's softened and tearful gaze. It had its effect.

'We need not settle the matter on the spot,' he suggested. 'Bear with me for a day or two, Aunt Yorke, so as to give me time to see a little more of my cousin and judge for myself.'

'To that there can be no objection, only you will not think it unreasonable that the time should not be unduly prolonged, and that you will give me a definite answer before you go?'

In this way the interview ended. Mrs. Yorke
had no reason to be dissatisfied with Gilbert's behaviour during the days that followed.

He saw, indeed, a great deal of Philippa; they
rode together, took walks together, and devoted the
evenings to music, for how else to abridge their
interminable length poor Gilbert did not know.
This, he said to himself, would be the sort of life
they would lead if they were married; and he
owned that it would be intolerable. During these
walks and rides he was the one who conversed,
having a store of experiences to fall back upon, and
a nimble wit in their recital; Philippa only listened.
When she questioned him at all, it was for details
of his recent illness, which was a subject he dis-
liked. Her voice was low and pleasant, and her
small, childlike face, lighted up by her sweet gray
eyes, was indescribably tender and wistful, but
there was a monotony of softness; no flashes of
intelligence responding to his own, none of the give
and take of swift mental intercourse which made o

Margery Denison the most delightful of companions, as well as the most adorable of women.

It was worse when she touched the piano as an accompaniment to his violin; after one or two melancholy attempts he released her from the task and himself from the torture it inflicted. He said, with a smile, 'All his performances should be solos.'

But this was hardly better: tingling with ardour or subdued to a divine tenderness, he met alike her gentle, undiscriminating smile, and could have groaned aloud in that anguish of exasperation which serves to qualify the privileges of the true artist. At such moments the remembrance of Margery's comprehension and eager sympathy turned the young fellow's heart sick within him.

Ah! in that letter to John Cartwright, written after his interview with Philippa's mother, he had miserably understated his case! For the reply to that letter he was waiting with feverish anxiety:

he had, as it were, staked his future on the cast of a die; he had agreed with himself that he would be bound by his friend's judgment.

It came duly, by return of post. Mrs. Yorke saw his colour change as he received it, and observed that he slipped it into his pocket without reading it, and that his interest in the breakfast-table therewith ceased.

As soon as he could escape observation, Gilbert went into the open air and put a considerable distance between himself and his aunt's house before he opened his cousin's letter. He had come unawares upon a little wood, and, following one of the tracks, found himself almost shut in by the silent, wintry trees, which were not yet so utterly bare but that the soft wind blowing through them brought down showers of their withering leaves. Sitting down upon a felled log, deep sunk in the long grass, now bleached and sere, and with the red and shrivelled bracken clustering at its feet, Gilbert prepared to meet the verdict he had challenged.

The letter was very short and the handwriting so clear that the reader mastered the contents almost at a glance.

Nature, in her simple and primitive forms, still worked strongly in Gilbert Yorke, maintaining a certain unsophisticated element beneath all the superficial culture that he had received. As he read, a little sharp cry escaped his lips, the letter dropped from his fingers, while a look of mingled protest and despair gave back to the young man's face the aspect which had been so familiar to it in the days of his boyish troubles. Presently he dropped his head upon his hands, with his elbows propped on his knees, and sat motionless, not so much thinking as suffering, till the sound of the neighbouring church clock striking the hour roused him from his stupor.

He got up slowly, but with evident determination, picked up the letter, glancing through it again before returning it to his pocket, and began slowly to retrace his steps towards the house.

'Poor old Jack,' he said to himself with a wistful tenderness, 'he knows everything under the sun except that one thing that alters all the values of life !'

Mrs. Yorke, keeping watch from the window of her morning-room, saw Gilbert return to the house, and her heart misgave her, for an unusual gravity and determination were apparent in his aspect. She heard him go up to his bedroom and turn the key in the lock—a proceeding which had, she thought, an ominous significance. Could he be packing up for departure before announcing to her the decision which she dreaded, but none the less expected ?

Her restlessness was so great that she could not sit still, but went downstairs to see how Philippa was employed, and whether Edward were established for the day.

She found the girl, who had a pretty taste for drawing, bent over her easel in the sunny window of the dining-room and looking, her mother thought, unusually pale and unattractive. There was a look of anxiety not to be mistaken in the heavy eyes and the drooping lines of the mouth, also in the eager movement with which she had turned as the door opened.

'Are you alone, dear?' she asked kindly. 'Where is Gilbert ?'

Philippa bent lower over her drawing, and her lips quivered.

Mrs. Yorke did not press the question, but went up to the easel and criticised the work with unusual indulgence, and with her hand resting on her daughter's shoulder.

'I must go now and see Ted,' she said briskly ; 'Gilbert will be looking for you directly. He went out after breakfast to enjoy his cousin's letter—I saw the post-mark. You know, I suppose, there is an absurd friendship between them ?' She smiled, nodded, and left the room.

In the hall she met Gilbert, and stopped to speak to him. How handsome he was, she thought, and

how well that air of quiet resolution became him !
She half wondered how any woman had been able
to resist him ; the expression in his brown eyes
struck her with a momentary reproach.

'Are you looking for Philippa ?' she asked cheer-
fully. 'She is in there,' indicating the room she
had left.

He coloured, made a gesture of assent, and would
have passed on, but she put her hand on his arm to
detain him.

'If,' she said in the lowest of tones, 'you propose to speak to her—of the future, let me beseech
you—because I am her mother and love her—not
to tell her what you have told me. Otherwise——'

Gilbert drew himself up with an air of acute
irritation.

'Excuse me, you must leave me alone in this
matter, or—you will frustrate yourself.'

He threw off her hand sharply and made a step
or two forward, when another thought struck him.

If he had made up his mind to offer himself as a victim to pity, or generosity, or family obligation, why should he not make the sacrifice graciously ?

He turned back to where his aunt still stood with knitted brows.

'I will tell Philippa nothing that can hurt her,' he said gently. 'I am bent on persuading her to be my wife.'

That night, in the quiet of his own room, Gilbert wrote to John Cartwright :

'It is all over, Jack, and you are responsible ! I stay here a day or two longer for decency's sake, and then go to Rookhurst. Try and join me there. If what I feel is the reward of virtue, commend me henceforth to the paths of vice ! There was never in me the stuff of which saints or martyrs are made.'

CHAPTER XIX.

Now and again in the relations between the sexes the question arises whether the woman should first reveal her love.

The pain and excitement that accompanied her father's death and the subsequent removal from The Chace were over, and Margery Denison and her aunt found a new phase of life opening before them. To both the death of Mr. Denison was a relief, unchecked by any regret except such as pity and magnanimity might bestow, and the change from the huge dilapidated mansion, with means totally inadequate to its suitable maintenance, to Mr. Cartwright's pretty house, produced that sense of security and independence which is so important a factor in the happiness of unmarried women.

Mrs. Sutherland, who had great zest for domestic arrangements and decoration, found inexhaustible interest in making The Hollies, as they had called their home, at once comfortable and elegant; she seemed, as Margery told her, to have renewed her youth, and the querulousness caused by an anxiety and irritability constantly suppressed, was replaced by the gentleness and sweetness of her natural temper.

The circumstance of Martin Cartwright being their landlord, and his son the chosen spiritual director of the elder lady, led of necessity to closer relations between the families than would at one time have seemed possible, and they were also now set free from those restrictions which the pride of another had imposed. Margery had called more than once at Elm Lodge to refer to Mrs. Cartwright some point of business, and on one of these occasions she had accepted her invitation to luncheon.

When John came in at dinner-time, it was to find her, as it were, at home in the house, more charming and *debonnaire* than he had ever known any woman before, and exercising over his mother that singular fascination which endowed her for the time being with a softness and sweetness new to his experience.

On other occasions the hospitality had been reversed, and Mrs. Sutherland had insisted on keeping John to a cup of afternoon tea, and Margery, coming in later from one of her long country rambles, radiant with health and exercise, had sat down to the fine old piano at her aunt's request, and by her delicate skill, and still more by the magic of her lovely voice, had renewed in the young minister's soul that passion of rapturous pain which had been first stirred by Gilbert's touch on his violin as a boy.

John held the conviction that if he had yielded

to this part of his nature, or circumstances had fostered his latent craving for this most subtle and subduing of sensuous delights, it would have shaken his fidelity both to duty and religion.

Now, as he sat in a dark corner of Mrs. Sutherland's pretty drawing-room, listening to the exquisite modulations of a voice whose common accent wrought in him a secret trouble, and with the face of the singer thrown into relief by the partial arrangement of the lights, his mood was that of a man mute under exquisite torture.

Margery was singing, to a more adequate setting than that popularly known, Tennyson's lyric, 'Tears, Idle Tears,' which is in itself a sort of apotheosis of the passion and despair of humanity, and when heard from the lips of a beautiful and adored woman—in vain adored—becomes endued with so trenchant a bitterness as to tax the endurance of any lover, however heroic.

When Margery had finished, herself strongly moved, silence fell on the little group. It needed a few moments' desperate struggle before John could trust his voice with speech, and then his acknowledgments were of the briefest. He excused himself to Mrs. Sutherland, and went away as soon as civility allowed.

But when he found himself outside the house in the welcome darkness of the wintry evening, he stood still for a few minutes and leaned heavily against the garden-gate, physically shaken by the force of the inward tumult. In the strained grasp and tightened lips were evidences of perilous intensity of nature, repressed by training and disciplined by grace, but still vital enough to challenge and defy the one and the other.

Truly love like this, when divorced from hope, is strong as death and cruel as the grave.

' My God ! how shall I bear it !' was the cry of his soul as he walked homeward.

Under this stress of feeling he walked rapidly, and had reached the gas-lamps at the entrance of the town sooner than he expected or desired. He was now within a short distance of Castle Street Chapel, and it occurred to his recollection that it was the weekly class night, and that he had promised to take the place of the class-leader in his absence.

For almost the first time in his mature experience his will revolted from the fulfilment of a religious duty; more, with the poet's words of passionate suggestion haunting his brain, which yet seemed inadequate to express his own hopeless yearning, and the image of Margery vivid to his eyes, for him to render the service required seemed mockery and outrage. He passed the chapel-door and walked on in the direction of his home. If he were not there, it would be concluded that he was unavoidably prevented, and someone else— someone more fit—would fill his place.

But before he had proceeded half-way he turned and retraced his steps. It was not that inclination had revived or that duty smiled upon him; it was rather her stern utterance as the voice of God that moved him, the remembrance that he had pledged himself to be her bondman, and the shame of shrinking from his post under the first assault of temptation. If a man were to serve God only when disposed to do so, where would be the fight or the victory?

After John was gone Mrs. Sutherland remarked:

'It seems strange, but I think Mr. Cartwright does not care for music. Perhaps he thinks it inconsistent with a Christian profession. I would not sing to him again, dear.'

Margery, who still kept her place at the piano, touched the keys in a dreamy impromptu and smiled. She had noticed the pallor of his face and the fire that burned in the depths of his sombre eyes, and her heart was singing quietly to itself for joy: 'He loves me, but he will not speak; how am I to give him the courage to speak?'

But the next time they met this conviction was shaken; there were no signs of strong feeling under stronger control. There was the friendship touched with deference to which he had accustomed her, that neither sought nor shunned intercourse, and which seemed to include her in his general attitude of benignity towards his fellow-creatures, an attitude which Margery promptly repudiated so far as she was personally concerned.

She went, as had become the custom, to Castle Street Chapel and listened attentively to his sermons, not, like her aunt, in the spirit of docile receptiveness, but in order to gather hints of mind and temper that might help her conclusions. They were not in any sense overwrought exhortations to an unreal or ascetic godliness, but they were permeated throughout with what may be held as the spirit of the age—that strong sense of the tie of human brotherhood and consequent ardour of sympathy which serve to reduce very materially the desire of personal happiness.

To a man absorbed in lessening the sum of misery and sin on the lines laid down by his Church, and who unconsciously revealed in the process treasures of fervour, pure-mindedness and spirituality, the contingent incidents of love or marriage seemed to form no part of the daily account.

Other opportunities of seeing him were difficult to obtain. She could scarcely offer herself as a guest at Elm Lodge, and he was always able to find some valid reason for excusing himself from Mrs. Sutherland's invitations, for, indeed, it was well known what a life of untiring work and effort he led.

On one occasion, indeed, Mrs. Cartwright, having met Margery in the Copplestone streets, referred to this subject (for the girl had almost a magnetic power of attracting sympathy), saying that she feared John worked too hard and was overtaxing a constitution he was mistaken in thinking one of cast-iron. She asked if either Mrs. Sutherland or herself had observed that he was looking thin and pale. To this Margery had replied that they had made no such observation; she had often remarked how much finer his face had become since he was a boy, and had concluded that it was an illustration of the shaping process to which mind was said to subject matter. And then she had added, with her delightful smile and direct, candid gaze : 'He grows more like you,' and Mrs. Cartwright had walked home with the glow of maternal pride at her heart and a deepened perception of Miss Denison's fascination.

Then on a sudden a pang smote her, a fear lest this charming young woman might step between herself and her son. It was a law of nature that, however fond and faithful a mother might be (only John little knew the depth of her devotion!), she was thrust aside and superseded by the despotic passion which a man conceived for the girl of his choice. If she found Margery Denison so attractive, was it not certain that John must do the same ? And if so ?

The notion distressed and repelled her. In such a case her son would pass out of her life in a sense,

and would leave her desolate with the cruel knowledge of a lost possibility. If she had been able to
draw him closer, to reveal the ardour of affection
she had held under such stern control, he might,
perhaps, have been content with what his home
gave him. But such compunction came too late.

It so happened that she sat up late for her son
that same evening: he was attending a circuit
meeting in a distant town, and the return train
was not due till midnight. Martin Cartwright and
the servants were gone to bed, for the mistress of
the house enjoyed a solitude that was cheered by
expectation, and she had the brightest of fires and
a dainty supper dish in readiness for the traveller's
refreshment. When he came she pleased herself
with waiting upon him, and she watched him, as
was too much her wont, with every faculty of
observation sharpened by the experiences of the
day.

She thought he had never seemed more sweet
and grateful, estimating her willing service beyond

its worth and seeming thoroughly appreciative of the blessings of his home. When supper was over they sat talking together over the incidents of the day; Mrs. Cartwright had a strong and enlightened interest in all matters relating to Church government, and John, though tired and depressed, did his best to meet it at every point. A little pause preparatory to separation had fallen between them. John was lying back in his father's chair, with his eyes fixed absently on the fire; and the mother, looking covertly towards him, feared that she detected in his aspect an air of sadness or dissatisfaction. An impulse seized her to try conclusions with her fate.

'John,' she asked quietly, though every pulse was beating hard, 'has the idea of marrying ever occurred to you? The time comes to most men when a mother's love and care do not meet all their wants.'

The question was so sudden and unexpected that he could not help a little start of surprise and the colour mounting to his face; but he had himself too well under control to betray any other signs of weakness.

'I do not think I shall ever marry,' was his answer. 'If new needs develop, mother, you must try and meet them.'

He got up to light his bedroom candle, and kissed her as he bade her good-night, which was not his habit or hers; but for all that Rachel Cartwright went to her room with a heavy heart. Love has a piercing insight, and in the expression of John's eyes she thought she read, not indifference, but renunciation.

Next day John obeyed his friend's summons, and went to Rookhurst, with a reluctance that nothing less than his love for Gilbert could have overcome.

He found him in a mood different from any that he had manifested before. For the first time John heard him speak harshly to a servant, and evince at all points an irritability foreign to his nature.

'I half repent, Jack,' he said to him, the evening of his arrival, as they sat after dinner over the wine and dessert, to which each was equally indifferent—'I half repent, Jack, I asked you to come. I did not know it, but I am unfit for society. I have done what you told me it was my duty to do, and the action won't bear reflection. I hate the prospect of the life before me—am not sure even now whether I shall be able to go through and keep my promise, and Rookhurst has become hateful, for it is for this that I have sold my soul! You do not speak ?' he added impatiently.

'I gave you what you asked for,' was John's answer, ' though it was against the grain, because it seemed cowardly to withhold an opinion for fear of the consequences. But you were your own master, and free to reject my advice. If I remember right, I only ventured to suggest that, as you were disappointed in your hopes of personal happiness, the next best thing was to try to make the happiness of somebody else, especially when

the doing so fell in with the hopes and plans of the
living and of the dead.'

'I am not of the temper to thrive on vicarious
happiness,' retorted the other, almost with a sneer.
'Have you ever tried it, Jack? To preach and to
practise are lines lying very far apart. To forego
the woman that you love is bad enough, but to
marry the one that you don't—by God, it shows
you possibilities in yourself that you have never
dreamed of before !'

John's eyes flashed. 'Then stop short before it
is too late. It will be infinitely better to break
your promise to your cousin now than to break her
heart hereafter ! Besides, pardon me, my poor
word would never have been given in favour of
your engagement had you not told me that there
was a difficulty not to be got over between you and
—Miss Denison.'

Gilbert laughed bitterly. 'Say it out, Jack !
There is no need to pick your words so carefully.
You mean, to be rejected is not to forego. Granted!

only I nurse the notion that the confession that I betrayed to you—could I ever in all my life keep anything back from you, old fellow?—was a pretence, a ruse of magnanimity to compel me to do what all my friends are persuaded it is my duty to do.'

' I think not,' said John sharply. ' Miss Denison would despise such a subterfuge. That she was magnanimous I agree, but it was the magnanimity that refused to spare herself in the desire to spare you.'

Gilbert pushed back his chair and rose impatiently.

' We will not talk of her, if you please ' — a suggestion to which the other only. too readily responded. ' Forgive me, old fellow, if I say that to hear you defend her is more than I can bear, and that to be the husband of Philippa Yorke will make me more than ever the lover of Margery. Even now it seems to me that I will have her for my own ! You know it, Jack ; she is part and parcel of my life.'

'Fetch your fiddle, Bert,' was the answer, 'and be the David to your own Saul! It is long since I heard it, and you will have brought back from Leipzig treasures new and old.'

Gilbert shook his head. 'It would be more than I dare; it would be like pouring vitriol on a wound, and bring all the exasperations of my lot close home; the girl I have promised to marry can scarcely distinguish one tune from another, while *she*——' He broke down in an agony of reminiscence.

'Even if she had lacked all that she has of beauty and wit and sweetness, I must have adored her, with a soul tuned as hers is to all the heights and depths of musical expression. How close at times we have lived together! Jack, old friend, do not despise me!'

John Cartwright went home heavy at heart.

CHAPTER XX.

' IT IS VERY GRIEVOUS !'

THE following winter was one of unusual severity over the whole continent of Europe, and in no part was its gloom and sternness felt more acutely than in the West Riding of Yorkshire. On the open moors round Copplestone the frozen snow which lay deep upon the ground showed not a trace of life upon its blackened surface; the shivering sheep had all been withdrawn within such shelter as the small farmers of the neighbourhood could provide, and no foot crossed the dreary wastes except under the pressure of necessity. Physical distress, the outcome of increased and unavoidable poverty, was rampant in the town, for the protracted frost, with its inevitable conditions, affected its staple industry, and the great factories were turning off half their hands. One or two mills also had closed their doors, and others were working only half-time, so that the ranks of the unemployed were swelled to an army mutinous with misery.

It was an aggravation of the wide-spread distress that day after day a dense fog enveloped the town, so that the very light of heaven was denied to those homes in which no food was found nor fire burned.

Private charity did its best to stimulate and support municipal organization until all the ordinary channels of relief were full of intelligent activity, without, as it seemed to the desponding, producing much appreciable result.

The Mayor of Copplestone, our old friend Martin Cartwright, with his sound sense, warm heart, and full purse, was at the head and front of every movement, and made for himself at this time a place in the esteem of his fellow-townsmen which it is given to few men to deserve. His son's place in the different schemes of energetic action was less prominent than his father's, but asked for more personal endurance and self-denial, for it meant an individual contact with want and misery under all its manifold aspects.

On one of these mornings of fog and frost Gilbert Yorke had come up from Rookhurst to attend a meeting summoned in the town-hall by the Mayor, for the discussion of a measure of relief which he was anxious to carry against a strong body of dissentients. He had come, not of his own accord, but in response to an urgent appeal for the support of his presence and purse from his cousin John; for although Gilbert was not indifferent to misery when brought under his notice, the impulse to seek in order to save was no part of his character.

The meeting being over in the sense desired by his uncle, and his own duty fulfilled by a munificent cheque, the young man felt himself at liberty to follow his inclinations, and they led him to pay a visit—long desired, but till now deferred, as much from a sense of danger as of duty—to the ladies at The Hollies.

As was to be expected from the state of the weather, he found them both at home, and was shown into the drawing-room, where Mrs. Sutherland was sitting busily engaged in some coarse needlework by the light of a reading-lamp. A low chair on the other side of the table, on which a garment in course of construction had been flung, bore witness, he thought, to recent companionship.

Mrs. Sutherland received him not only with kindness, but effusion, pouring forth those friendly inquiries so welcome to an anxious guest.

' Why had he been so long in coming to see them ? Could he stay to luncheon ? What did he think of their new house ? And where had he found inducement enough to exchange Rookhurst for Copplestone in such weather as this ?'

Gilbert accepted her invitation and answered her

questions with eagerness; her pleasant cordiality had warmed his heart, and his own supreme anxiety had been set at rest by the sound of Margery's delicious voice on the stairs trilling an air from one of the most graceful and popular of comic operas. He observed a start of surprise as she entered and recognised him, and this quickened the current of excitement in his own nerves.

'Am I welcome?' he asked, as he rose to meet her and held her hand for a moment in both his own.

'Our friends are always welcome,' was her answer. 'But on such a day!'

He explained while she sat down at the table and resumed her sewing, asking him questions about the meeting with an interest which surprised him.

'Do not let us talk about it any more,' he said at last. 'I am ashamed how cold my philanthropy is. To give money is to give so little, and yet I feel quite unfit for personal service. That does not seem your case, Margery. I never remember seeing you working with a needle before, and that rough woollen frock must be for a poor child.'

'It *is* rough,' she answered, exhibiting it. 'But I dared not dispute Mrs. Cartwright's judgment. The head-quarters of our local charities are at Elm Lodge, and we all take our orders from there— don't we, auntie ? We are being taught that nothing counts but personal service.'

'Ah,' he said, smiling, 'I perceive that you begin to know my cousin very intimately.'

The light of the unseasonable lamp was falling full upon Margery's face, and as Gilbert sat near her, and was watching her attentively, he could not help seeing that the words he had spoken so lightly brought a sudden flush of colour to her cheek, and that the needle trembled in her fingers.

At the same moment Mrs. Sutherland was summoned out of the room for a consultation with her cook, whose mind was exercised on the subject of luncheon, having heard that the master of Rookhurst was to be their guest.

When Margery in her turn looked at Gilbert, she was startled by the change in his appearance. He had become very pale, and his attitude had the rigidity of one who has received an unexpected shock.

'My God!' he said at last, under his breath, 'can this be true?'

He made a movement as if he would have risen from his seat, but the room was too encumbered with furniture to admit of the resource of walking about in it, and he sat down again, shading his face with his hand.

For a few moments Margery pursued her sewing as if in defiance of her agitation; then, throwing it down, she rose and walked towards the fireplace, standing on the hearth with her clasped hands hanging loosely before her, her head a little bowed, and her gaze fixed on the ground in intense cogitation.

Presently she raised her head proudly, and turned so that she could see her companion.

' Well ?' she demanded. ' Well ? You have surprised my secret, and I am not ashamed ! He is
your dearest friend—what have you to say to
me ?'

Gilbert neither spoke nor stirred. Margery, with
a vague sense of alarm, went up to him and touched
his shoulder.

' Are we not friends ?' she asked, in a voice of
melting kindness. ' Half my secret was yours
before ; you are welcome to the other half. Answer
your own question ! Tell me—not if he is worthy,
but if you think me worthy ?'

Still he kept the same posture and the same
silence. Margery withdrew her hand.

' You frighten me,' she said in an altered tone.
' You have had your answer from my lips long ago ;
you are pledged to your cousin, as indeed honour
and generosity compelled, and yet—is it grievous to
you that he whom I love is the man that you love
best in the world ?'

' Yes,' he said, at last lifting up his face,

which looked haggard with misery, 'it is very grievous!'

'I do not quite understand,' she answered, and yet her eyes were full of tender sympathy. 'I remember what you were as a boy, when we first knew each other, how patient and sweet and heroic, and so I have proved you ever since; you cannot belie your nature and turn disloyal at a stroke! Is not John Cartwright your dear friend? Would you have me believe your love for him—shall I dare to say your love for me?—was of that poor sort that it would withhold the happiness that it does not bestow?'

'I do not justify myself,' he said; 'you have always thought better of me than I deserve. I cannot touch the height of wishing that any man other than myself should make you happy.'

'Not even the man who loves you as his own soul—who has urged your claims and merits upon me again and again with an ardour that I doubt if he will ever use in his own behalf!'

'I doubt it too! Will it be possible for him to plead for what he knows has been denied to me, or to build up his happiness on the ruin of mine? Is there no loyalty to be looked for on the one side as on the other? If John Cartwright is what you think him—no, I will say more!—*since* he is what you think him, it is morally impossible that he can do this thing.'

Margery turned a little pale, then she said deliberately, with a sort of noble boldness:

'I had not sufficiently thought of all this—it is a difficulty to be got over only in one way. It will rest with you to remove this stumbling-stone. *You* must make John Cartwright free to speak.'

She neither blushed nor faltered as she said this, but met his eyes fully, with an expression that seemed to challenge him to make good her estimate of himself.

'You ask me,' was his answer, 'what no woman ought to ask of the man who loves her. Besides, you do not yet understand. It is true, as you say, that

I am pledged to my cousin Philippa, and while I mean to keep faith, my prayer day and night has been for deliverance. I have been fool enough to cheat myself with the notion that you cast me off out of pity for her and for my fortune, and that some turn of fate would bring us together. Life as it is has only been bearable under this madness of credulity. Now it is brought home to me that I have really lost you—beyond redemption—and that I owe such loss to my dearest friend. Margery, to do what you require of me would be to give you more than my life!'

'Well, if so,' she said in a suppressed, passionate voice, 'I demand even that sacrifice. 'I would have loved you if I could, God knows! but you must see that, even in that case, difficulties would have existed hard to overcome. Those between us now are insurmountable, and it behoves you to submit. You say you love me. I ask you to help me to be happy, and I know you better than you know yourself.'

She stopped, but as he did not answer, she went on :

' Who is better acquainted than you with what my life has been from a child? What examples have been set me, and to what influences have I been exposed? I think I love John Cartwright because the simplicity and unselfishness of his character seem, from force of contrast, to offer me what I desire most. I do not mean he has no higher claims, but it is not his gifts which attract me. He saved my life—you will understand now —but it was not the action but the unconsciousness of it that won me. As a friend, speaking of you, he has touched my heart as no one has ever done before.'

She paused again, her head erect and her aspect instinct with tender animation. This time Gilbert spoke.

'I can well believe it,' he said, with a groan ; ' only spare me if you can. What is the service that I am to render you—or him? You know

that he loves you ? But that follows of necessity.'

She turned aside to hide the blushes that
crimsoned her face ; then, recovering her firmness :

'I do not *know*, although my belief is strong.
No word or look has passed between us, but have
you not yourself shown me that his lips are
righteously closed until you give him leave to open
them ? I trust you, Gilbert, as I would trust no
one else in the world, because I have proved you a
hundred times before—I trust you with my pride,
my honour as a woman. Take care !' she continued more tremulously. 'Do not offer what he
does not want—tell him no more than that he is
free to seek.'

'You try me very hard,' he answered. 'It is
almost more than I can bear—this solicitude to
win what I have poured out at your feet like water,
and in vain ! Will any friendship stand such a
test ? You will leave me nothing !'

He took up his hat and turned to depart.

'I cannot stay—excuse me to Mrs. Sutherland.'

Then, having reached the door, he came back again, noting the attitude of dejection she had involuntarily assumed, and that her eyes were full of tears—not for herself, he knew, but for him.

'I promise,' he said, touching her hand, 'to do the thing you wish, and if it be baldly or bluntly done, you will understand and—forgive me. Besides, what matters ?   The result must be the same.'

And he departed.

CHAPTER XXI.

It was the morning of Christmas Day, but the family at Fair Lawns were by no means in a mood congenial to the sacred season. The weather was so intensely cold as to nip the energies of all but the most vigorous and light-hearted, and neither Mrs. Yorke nor her children belonged to this category.

The intention had been to have entertained a party of intimate friends for the Christmas week to meet the young master of Rookhurst, and to give the opportunity for congratulation on the engagement of the daughter of the house. Publicity had already been secured to this event by the efficacious means of inserting a carefully-studied paragraph in the leading society papers, which was perused with great satisfaction by the old lawyer, Mr. Percival, to whom Mrs. Yorke had caused copies to be sent, and by Gilbert himself (who had been made the subject of the same postal attention) with feelings of hopeless dejection.

He had accepted, as in duty bound, his aunt's invitation for Christmas, and then had written again a day or two after to explain that he had slipped on the ice in skating, and so seriously sprained his knee that he should not be able to keep his engagement. His doctors gave him no hope of leaving the sofa for a month to come.

Mrs. Yorke was unreasonably angry; she was almost disposed to regard the excuse as mendacious, and, when convinced to the contrary, revolved in her mind the possibility of sending Philippa to play nurse to her cousin, but relinquished the idea as impracticable. The result was that she refrained from issuing her invitations, and, as we have said, Christmas Day arose on a depressed family group. The only alleviation was a present from Gilbert Yorke to his *fiancée* in the shape of a gold Venetian necklace of exquisite workmanship. Mrs. Yorke, while allowing this, pronounced the gift to be very much below the occasion in point of value.

Philippa, however, was perfectly satisfied. In the privacy of her own room she kissed the pretty trinket with tender enthusiasm, and took the case which contained it in her pocket to church, feeling a secret consolation in clasping it covertly in her hand during the duller portions of the service. On her return she made her toilet with many a fond regret that Gilbert would not be there to admire her new frock, fastened the necklace about her slender throat, and then went down to her brother's room to exhibit the gift.

Edward, who was always most sullen and irritable on anniversaries, welcomed his sister on this occasion with a sort of avidity. There was, indeed, a curious excitement and animation in his manner. He examined the chain minutely, pronouncing it in the most contemptuous manner to be 'nothing but trumpery.'

'Where is the fellow hiding all the family diamonds?' he asked. 'Don't you think something of that sort would have been more appropriate for the future mistress of Rookhurst?' And then he began to laugh with that curious lack of congruity and restraint which is one of the most aggravating indications of weakness of mind.

'I like it better than anything else he could have sent me!' Philippa protested loyally. 'What is there to laugh at, Ted?'

He continued to laugh, and the girl, turning away from his couch, sat down in a low chair by the fire, and leaned her head on her hand. Her own spirits were depressed by disappointment, and there seemed an element of mockery in her brother's laughter which gave it more significance than usual, and fretted her nerves. The daylight was already fading, and the early dusk of a cloudy winter's day shadowed the room, the leaping flames on the open hearth throwing into relief the small girlish figure in its crimson cloth frock, and the pathetic pose of the bowed head.

Edward glanced towards her, conscious of an ill-understood influence from the sweetness and purity of his sister's aspect. He ceased to laugh, and raised himself on his elbow.

'There are many worse-looking girls than you,' he said in his harsh, rasping voice, 'and though I owe you no mercy on the score of your selfish meanness in playing into this fellow's hands, I am half sorry for you too. As for him, it's of a piece with his infernal insolence that he has dared to treat you as he has done. Didn't I promise you from the beginning, Phil, that I would spoil your little game?'

Philippa looked up anxiously. Gilbert's name was never mentioned in Edward's hearing without provoking a torrent of abuse, but there was an eagerness and intention in his present manner that raised a vague alarm.

'What do you mean?' she asked, her soft appealing eyes full of tears. 'Why can't you let Gilbert alone? What fresh cause of offence has he given you? I suppose nothing new has happened since he was here last?'

Edward writhed on his couch after a fashion of his own when under strong excitement, uttering at intervals a low decisive chuckle which irritated even Philippa's meek spirit beyond endurance.

'I cannot bear it,' she exclaimed passionately, and, going to her brother's couch, she put her hand on his shoulder as if to restrain his movements, and shook him with her gentle strength. 'Be quiet, Ted!' she entreated. 'You know how mother hates to see you behave like that.'

The unaccustomed check was not to be endured.

'How dare you!' he shouted, throwing off her hand viciously. 'Who are you to teach me how to behave myself?—little fool as you are, to think that Cousin Yorke or any other man would ever care for your baby face! I had meant to break the fall for you, but you may take it now as you can get it. Look here! Read that!'

His hand had been for some time in the depths of his pocket, and he now drew forth a folded paper and thrust it towards her. For a moment the girl regarded it as if it had been a scorpion prepared to sting, then, unconsciously influenced by an authoritative gesture from her brother, she slowly extended her hand and took it.

'Open and read!' he commanded. 'Stir up the fire, there will be light enough.'

As if under a spell, she did as she was told, sitting down again in the chair she had just quitted, for her limbs trembled under her.

The paper which her brother had given her to examine consisted of a portion of a letter, and was in the well-known handwriting of Gilbert Yorke. It had the appearance of having been torn across and crushed together, probably before

being flung aside; but the creases had been carefully smoothed out, and the rent neatly joined
together with a strip of adhesive paper. Philippa
glanced at the first words, and flushed with indignation.

'It is addressed to his cousin, John Cartwright
—do you think I will read it?'

'You will either read it, miss, or hear it from
my lips. I know it by heart. Fletcher found it
when he moved the writing-table in his room a
day or two ago, and brought it to me. He has
had my orders, and knows they are worth minding.
Since then I've bided my time.'

He stopped a moment, for his voice was getting
beyond his control, and he was anxious not to be
overheard by his mother. Her meddling would
spoil his revenge.

'Look here, Phil,' he resumed with an eagerness painfully repressed, 'I want to make you
understand. Don't you remember when he was
here last he got a letter from the draper's son,

and popped directly after? Don't you remember? Mother told me all about it! Who knows but you what blasted lies he told you, damning his soul for the sake of Rookhurst, under the canting advice of the Methodist parson!'

He had raised himself by degrees almost into a sitting posture, but at this point he threw himself back as if exhausted.

'God knows,' he muttered, 'I always hated him; 'but even I scarcely thought he was such a black-guard as he is!'

Still Philippa held the letter in her hand, with her eyes turned resolutely away and distended with misery.

Then Edward began in a voice of insufferable mockery to recite the words aloud, 'Dear old Jack,' but the girl clapped her hands to her ears to shut out the sound.

'Don't! You will drive me mad. Rather than that I will read it. Is it about me?' piteously.

'Rather! Poor little fool!'

The touch of tenderness in his voice broke down her power of further resistance; she let her eyes dwell on the letter, and grasped its meaning in an agony of apprehensiveness.

It was the first draft of Gilbert's letter to John Cartwright, which he had torn across and flung aside because it had seemed to him too harsh and outspoken.

It is unnecessary to give phrases; the burden was simply this :

He was coerced by circumstances into marrying one woman when he adored another : could the belief that his cousin loved him, or the duty he owed to his grandfather, justify a step that was repugnant to every instinct and conviction of his nature, and must result in the misery of both? In the extremity to which his aunt's action had reduced him, he seemed to have lost the power of personal decision, and he had decided to act as John Cartwright should advise.

Philippa let the paper flutter from her hand to

the floor, and had turned to fly from the room to hide the shame that almost consumed the sense of misery; but she was standing near enough to her brother for him to grasp the folds of her gown, and he caught and detained her.

'What will you do?' he asked sharply. 'What will you do? You do not go till you tell me that!'

Philippa struggled to be free, but finding it impossible, faced the necessity with a resolution and a dignity that even Edward recognised.

'What shall I do?' she repeated. 'What can a girl do who is so miserable and disgraced as I am, but give him back his word and set him free?' And then, with a sudden bitter cry, she sobbed out: 'Oh mother, mother!'

Edward dropped back on his couch with his eyes fixed on her face; there was something in its aspect that pierced through his selfish callousness.

'Poor soft little fool!' he said, but not unkindly. 'I was half afraid you would stick to your bargain in order to give the fellow what he wanted. But—you have not reckoned with mother.'

Philippa made a gesture of distress.

'She could not force me, and—if she tried it would be of no use. Oh, let me go!'

He released his hold, and the girl fled into her own room, and, locking the door, flung herself prone upon the rug before the fire in an agony of distress and humiliation.

Half an hour ago she had been full of quiet content and joy. She had never been so presumptuous as to expect that Gilbert's feeling for her was as hers for him. Was it possible? she had asked herself. But she was quite content to accept his affectionate kindness as an equivalent for her devotion, and to trust to its influence to win a warmer regard. Indeed, so strong was her sense of her own deficiencies, that she would scarcely have dared to accept the offer he had made her had she not been aware that it was in her power to enrich the man she loved. This had

given her confidence, and perhaps had prevented
her from analyzing too curiously the motives which
had led to the end she desired. She had also in
her almost childish simplicity deceived herself by
thinking that no one, except perhaps her mother,
guessed her secret, an opinion in which that mother,
aware of her sensibility, had taken pains to confirm her; while the many conclusive proofs which
Gilbert had given of his indifference to wealth and
position led her to the comforting conviction that
he would never have asked her to be his wife had
he not cared enough for her to think that they
might be happy together. That their grandfather's
wishes weighed a little in the account was only
natural and right, and she was grateful for this
help to her felicity.

But now she saw clearly—saw how she had
deceived herself, and that what she had joyfully
welcomed as a free-will offering had been, in fact,
the outcome of coercion and sacrifice. He not
only did not care for her, but he cared passion-

ately for someone else—someone, doubtless, better fitted to be his mate, whose merits would aggravate his sense of her own shortcomings. He had offered himself in defiance of despair and wretchedness—under pressure from her mother—based on an appeal to his pity for herself, and under the conviction that marriage would mean misery for both.

For a time Philippa lay on the floor suffering in silent misery, for the thought was present to her mind that if she gave herself the relief of sobs and tears she would be unable to keep her secret from her mother; but after a time she roused herself from this attitude of humiliation and sat down in a chair by the fire, with her aching head on her hand, and her pale face beginning to flush and her eyes to kindle as thought and resolution pressed upon her.

'I thank God,' she said to herself, 'that I know in time—that it is not too late! How should I have lived my life if we had married and I had found it out afterwards!'

There was a knock at the door, and a maid entered to say that Mrs. Yorke was waiting for luncheon. Her first impulse was to excuse herself, but she corrected it on second thoughts, and sent back word that she would come immediately. As soon as she was alone again she arranged her hair and dress, and then stood for a moment, frail but resolute, to consider her plan of action.

Before going to the dining-room she had decided to speak to her brother again; therefore she ran swiftly downstairs and turned aside at once to his room. The table by the side of his couch was set for luncheon, and Fletcher was already in attendance; but Philippa's purpose was too fixed to be easily daunted.

'Leave me alone with my brother for a minute,' she said. 'I want to speak to him privately;' and the man obeyed at once before Edward could interfere, won by the sweet authority of her manner. Then she went up to the couch and put her hand gently on her brother's arm. 'I want you to make me a promise, Ted. Do not tell mother what you have told me—to-day, at all events.'

Her voice was low and controlled, but her manner conveyed the idea of strenuous entreaty. He pushed away her hand with his usual rough impatience.

'I do nothing in the dark. Will it help my purpose or hinder it?'

Philippa paused to swallow the sob that rose in her throat.

'You can judge for yourself. I want to write to Gilbert to break off our engagement before—before——' She stopped.

Edward looked at her with keen suspicion.

'Can I trust you? Will you really do what you say? If so, I will hold my tongue of course, and more—I will take care that Fletcher posts the letter on the sly. Bring your letter to me,' he continued, growing excited, as was his wont. 'I am your brother, and have a right to be consulted.

I am afraid of you, Phil; you have been crying over that—blackguard !'

'Oh, he is not that,' she said, with a little smile. 'But you would never understand. He meant to do right. I can't show you my letter, but I will tell you what I mean to say. There is only one thing possible.'

She drew herself away from him for a moment, and spoke again after a moment's struggle for self-control.

'I mean to tell him the truth—it will be the best way. I shall tell him we have found the copy of that letter, and that, now I know, I set him free from his promise and would not marry him for any consideration on earth.'

And then, falling suddenly on her knees by her brother's side and hiding her face on his arm, she added:

'Ted, need our mother know at all—that is, the whole truth ? She will be so angry with him, and will try to make him suffer for it if she can.'

For the second time that day a movement of
pity and tenderness touched the young man's
heart, and, perhaps for the first time in his life,
he attempted a caress. He put his hand on his
sister's bowed head and stroked her hair affectionately.

'Poor soft little thing!' he answered; 'he has
flouted you, but you don't want him hurt! So
much the greater scoundrel he.' Then, pushing
her away: 'Look sharp and get your letter written,
and bring it here. It is Christmas Day, and I
shall have to send Fletcher into town—it won't do
to risk its lying all night in the village post-office.'

She rose suddenly, hearing Mrs. Yorke's voice,
and was hurrying out of the room, when he called
her back.

'On your honour, Phil? But a girl has no
honour! You refuse to marry Gilbert Yorke and
to give him—Rookhurst?'

He broke into a low chuckle, waiting for her
answer with malice glowing in his eyes.

The girl's slight figure seemed to dilate; an indefinable expression touched her lips.

'On my honour, as before God,' she said solemnly, 'I will never marry my cousin, Gilbert Yorke!'

CHAPTER XXII.

HIS LOSS SHALL NOT BE MY GAIN.

IT was midnight. John Cartwright sat in his bed-room at his writing-table with an open letter before him—one that he had read and re-read since its receipt, but which still remained unanswered. During this interval he had gone about his daily work like a man to whom something has happened, changing the focus and bearings of life.

A reading-lamp stood on the table, by which light rather than that of gas John always preferred to work, and he had fallen into the habit of doing all work of brain or pen after the rest of the household were asleep. The fire had burnt itself out, although the weather—a week before Christmas—was in-

tensely cold, but the young minister had not noticed
it. He was sitting with his forehead propped on
his hands and his eyes fixed on the letter before
him, to which, he had said to himself, an answer
should be written before he slept.

Presently, with a deep breath of oppression, he
pushed back his chair, moved by the instinctive
impulse to help the activity of the mind by bodily
movement, but he checked it. To walk his room at
night would be certain to attract his mother's
anxious vigilance, and for a moment his brows
contracted with a sense of impatience under restraint. It was one of those trivial circumstances
which serve at times to fire a train of impressions.

A vision rose before him : a home of his own
where freedom reigned, presided over and inspired
by a woman whose look and voice and touch,
which now thrilled and disordered every perception,
would then become the channels of such peace
and joy as are only glimpsed in dreams ; one
with whom the outward endowments of beauty and

distinction were of less account than a freshness and charm of character which endeared and ennobled every grace and gift.

A woman whom many men had loved in vain, and who by a curious exercise of feminine perversity—if such a word could be applied to a generosity that dissolved his soul in gratitude—had turned from the great and the greatly endowed to bestow the treasure of her love upon his own insignificance. It was not to be believed—not, at least, to be understood. If accepted, in spite of reason and conviction, it would serve to revolutionize his life and nature. The husband of Margery Denison could never be the same man as the son of Rachel Cartwright, or adhere to the plan of life he, as such, had marked out for himself; and yet the life so marked out was the issue of the most deliberate purpose.

Nor was this all, nor chief.

To seize and drink this draught of intoxication offered to him meant to take for himself the trea-

sure on which Gilbert Yorke had staked and lost
his hopes of happiness. True, the possession of it
having been denied him, he had consented to
accept his fate and to order his future life on other
and alien lines, but how false to all the dues of
honour must that man be who could build up a
home of ideal blessedness upon the ruins of his
friend's !

Margery Denison as John's wife would stand for
ever as a barrier between them, however gallant
might be the struggle to overleap it on the one part
or the strength of the desire on the other.

John Cartwright turned back to read once more
the concluding phrases of the letter in which, with
the utmost delicacy and consideration, Gilbert
Yorke had told him that the man who stood
between himself and the woman that he worshipped
was the friend whom he least suspected and loved
best in the world.

'At the first shock, Jack—I suppose because it
was so unexpected—the fact that it was *you* who

were my rival seemed a cruel aggravation of the case. It was like a blow from a beloved hand! But that feeling passed, and now I am prepared to say, Go in boldly, and take the happiness of which, I own, I am not half so worthy. We will nct meet for a little while, but in the long-run things shall be as before between us. I cannot afford to lose my friend as well.'

There was a postscript, after Gilbert's manner.

'Write soon, and tell results. I shall have more courage to go to Philippa when all is settled.'

And it was an answer to this letter which still remained unwritten.

When at length it was achieved it was very brief, and to this effect :

'I propose to go to The Hollies to-morrow. I will write to you after I have seen Miss Denison.'

For John Cartwright had come at length to a conclusion—namely, that it would be an unmanly and ignominious thing to carry out the purpose that had slowly taken root in his mind without going to the woman he loved, and granting to her loving-kindness the poor comfort of confession and explanation.

To carry this out would be a task of such difficulty that he spent the sleepless night in preparation for it, and arose the next morning after an experience so searching that it left its traces equally in the pallor of his set face and the increased determination of his soul.

It was impossible that a love and an intelligence like Rachel Cartwright's should perceive these indications and not suspect a secret meaning in them ; but life was teaching her those lessons which are never finally shut against the sincere in heart, and she had the grace not only to keep silence, but to show no signs of comprehension.

Margery was seated at the piano when John Cartwright was announced, for the maid, knowing his intimacy with the family, had taken him at once into the room. She rose abruptly, with a sudden rush of sweet womanly shames and perturbations such as no other man's name had ever excited.

The hour was unconventionally early for a call, and the thought that flashed across her mind was radiant with the conviction of the motive that had brought him. Gilbert had been loyal! When was he ever otherwise? That John Cartwright looked pale, with a concentrated passion in the depths of his dark eyes, only confirmed her impression, but she was willing to trifle with her happiness.

'Listen!' she said, after the first somewhat formal greeting, 'I have been practising this impromptu of Chopin — does it commend itself to you?'

There was no resource but to listen. He stood by the piano at the back of her chair while her skilled fingers gave a magical interpretation to the complex subtlety of the piece she had chosen, but when she had finished he did not break the silence.

'I see! You do not like it?' she said, turning towards him with a smile.

'No; but I am no judge, only my feeling is that music like that is in a sense immoral. It seems to dissolve the power of the will: there is no appeal or aspiration in it like—Beethoven or Bach. It is sensuous, and only that. I speak as a fool, under correction,' he added, smiling; 'for I know nothing but what my cousin Gilbert has taught me.'

'He has taught you very well,' was her answer. 'I suppose no one ever yet suggested that Chopin's art was calculated either "to raise a mortal to the skies, or draw an angel down." But you can scarcely desire that the attitude of the mind should be always that of aspiration? This would be to tax poor human nature too severely — though perhaps that is your fault, Mr. Cartwright?'

She looked at him as she spoke with that expression of veiled tenderness which changed the playful reproach almost into a caress. John, in his agony of self-containment, could have groaned aloud. Then he said:

'I am anxious to tell you why I have come so early this morning. May I hope we shall not be interrupted?'

'We are safe from interruption,' she answered, getting up from the piano, and sitting down in a low chair by the fire with her back to the light. The winter daylight was not very searching, but Margery feared lest her face should betray her, and she had caught a vague apprehension from the tones of his voice.

'We shall not be interrupted,' she repeated, a little mechanically; 'for my aunt is writing letters for the Indian mail in her own room.'

John approached the fire also, and stood opposite to her. The position showed every line of his face and figure, and before he had spoken a word she saw it was his purpose to renounce her. But she also saw that he loved her, therefore she would be able to shake his resolution. He stood for a few moments motionless, with his eyes on the ground, as if seeking for the right words; then he looked up, and—not to spare himself like a coward—he looked at her as he spoke.

'I want to tell you in as few words as I can what has brought me here this morning. I am unfit for work or duty until I have spoken to you, so it seemed best to lose no time in doing so. I only trust—humbly—that I shall not make you angry.'

'I do not think you will do that.'

'Do you remember,' he began, after another pause of reflection, 'that I was with my cousin, Gilbert Yorke, when he first met you and your father in Copplestone? You stopped your carriage to speak to him—but it is scarcely likely you should remember.'

'I remember perfectly.'

'I was then as dull and loutish a boy as any in all Yorkshire, but from that moment a new sense quickened in my soul. I saw something adorable, and—I adored it; at first almost as unconsciously as the green blade shoots under the sun. My cousin, too, did much to help me at this time. Since then circumstances, as you know, have arisen which brought us into contact. I have learnt to know you intimately, but I have no words to explain fitly all that this means to me : one thing it means, which I am bound to confess before I put it out of my life. I have dared to love you, Miss Denison.'

' Then, if you love me—and I know that you love me—why must you put this love out of your life ?'

She raised her eyes and looked at him—eyes in which reproach and tenderness were at strife ; then she added, with a delightful smile and an accent hard to resist :

' Are you afraid that I could not make you happy ? I would try very hard.'

John glanced at her, then looked away and set his face as a flint. Such was his secret passion, that he could have grovelled at her feet and kissed the hem of her gown ; could have surrendered duty and friendship to taste the delirious delights of their mutual love. It was the very extremity of his condition that gave the harshness to look and voice under which Margery instinctively shrank.

'Yes,' he said; 'I am afraid, rather I am sure, that we could not be happy together. I can scarcely believe that you care for me, but if you do it is from some impulse of generosity for which I shall be grateful to my life's end, but which could not stand the test of union. We have been born and bred in a different sphere, and my intimate associations are those which you have been taught—I will not say to despise, but to consider as beneath you. And they are beneath you! Personally, I should disappoint and offend you in many ways. Put to the proof, no effort of high-mindedness on your part could prevent the shock of alienation which my inevitable short-comings would produce ——'

She interrupted him.

'Why, this is the grace of self-depreciation run mad! What you say might have held—in a little measure—if you had been other than a gentleman or I a lady of high degree, instead of all but a poor dependent on my good aunt's bounty! You will have to find weightier reasons than these before I shall consent "to be put out of your life."'

'Oh,' he cried sharply, 'spare me too much kindness! What am I to say? I adore you beyond reason and religion; and yet to ask you to be my wife is a madness against which, blinded as I am, I will struggle to defend myself. Do you know what it would mean to me? It would mean to lay down the duties to which I am pledged, for such service as I owe would be incompatible with my feeling for you. It would mean besides to spoil my mother's life; she loves me so closely that it would hurt her beyond healing to know that her love was no longer necessary and influential.'

'And since when,' asked Margery indignantly, and rising as she spoke, 'since when has it been held a man's duty to sacrifice the woman he loves to the selfishness of his mother or his own infirmity of purpose? If this be all, you may trust me to brighten, not to impoverish, your mother's life. I will make all her hopes and cares and aspirations mine, and will follow you so closely in your daily duties, let them be what they may, that neither she nor her son shall find any flaw in my humility or my devotion. I think you do not believe that I love you.'

'I believe it,' he answered, but with his eyes turned away from the allurement of her face; 'or how else could I explain such matchless generosity? But I repeat—forgive me—that it is not me—such as I am—that you love, but some idea of an exalted imagination. I would not take advantage of your noble error, and endure the agony and shame of watching your awakening, even if nothing else divided us.'

'And what else divides us,' she demanded, 'beyond your mother and your absolute distrust of my loyalty and judgment?'

'The reasons I have alleged are enough,' he replied, with a desperate firmness, 'although you do not see fit to render them right. But—you must know it—were all else equal, I would not take the happiness with which you dazzle me because—I am Gilbert Yorke's friend.'

'Ah,' she said, with a deep breath, 'it is as I feared! And yet I hoped you were above it! You mean that you think it right to sacrifice two lives for the sake of a scruple that will not even benefit the man for whom it is made? Is it worth while? I am as far off from Gilbert Yorke as if he had already married his cousin, or I—if I dare say it— had become your wife. You would put me to shame, only I know that you are arguing against yourself, and I am not of the sort that will give their happiness the go-by for a delusion!'

Under this appeal John stood mute. She could

perceive that he was suffering acutely, almost beyond his endurance, and it was because she was so sure of her power over him that she played her part with such tender boldness. It was, however, not to argument, but to her personal influence, she must trust.

'John,' she said softly, 'give up this useless struggle. Let us be happy.'

He could not resist the magnetism of her voice and look. For the first time during the interview he came close up to her, and, taking her hands, strained them against his heart with eyes full of passion and despair.

'There is not a word to be said nor a plea to urge on the side of yielding to this bliss you offer that I have not weighed and pondered even to exhaustion, and I have decided against them all. Not in such moments as these, or I must have yielded, but last night—alone—with God and my conscience. Dear, it is labour lost to say over again what I have already said so ineffectually,

but my purpose is fixed. To have you for my wife
is not for me. Some men have grace to love their
wives and serve God and their neighbour as before.
I could not, for my nature is hard to keep in
bounds, and love is not to me a holy affection, but
an idolatry that would make of me a traitor. Nor,
in spite of your divine confidence, would you escape
the disappointment I have foretold. This is
enough without thought of Gilbert, and that
thought is enough without any other. The want
of your love has blasted his life, and to him I owe,
in a sense, the salvation of mine. His loss shall
never be my gain.'

Long before he had finished speaking he had
recovered his firmness, and had dropped the hands
he had clasped so eagerly. Margery stood erect
without any attempt at interruption, her lovely
eyes looking straight into his with an expression of
sorrow rather than of anger.

'I cannot plead any more,' she said, when he
had ceased speaking; 'you must go your own way,

only—you deceive yourself! You do not love me.'

He hesitated a moment, then decided to let the interpretation stand.

' I will go,' was his answer, ' for I know not what more to say except that, though I shall never marry, I shall hold all women dear for your sweet sake. I thank God, even as it is, that I have been permitted to know you. Farewell.'

He refrained from all mockery of leave-taking, and had turned to depart, but Margery stretched out her hand with tears in her eyes.

' One word more. You do this in obedience to your cousin's action ? I know he loved me nobly, but not nobly enough to be willing that I should be happy in my own way.'

John grasped the extended hand. ' I cannot trust myself to explain,' he said, ' but I will leave you this.'

He drew Gilbert's letter out of his pocket and put it on the table beside her.

'It will teach you to know Gilbert better.'

Then he bowed his head, and for one passionate moment pressed his lips close against the hand that he still held. The next Margery heard the house door close upon him.

CHAPTER XXIII.

WEIGHED, BUT NOT FOUND WANTING.

Ten days after John Cartwright's interview with Margery Denison, Gilbert paid one of his rare visits to Elm Lodge. It had become a custom when the friends wanted to meet that John should give himself a holiday by going to Rookhurst.

Life often seems to repeat itself. It was just such a day of gloom and fog as when the boy had first made his unfamiliar journey from his uncle's shop to his house, and the latter was gas-illumined now as then. Also, when Gilbert entered the dining-room, the recollection of that time was brought back vividly to his mind.

No alteration had been made in the apartment:

the furniture stood precisely in the same places—Mrs. Cartwright not being bitten by the tarantula of change; the fire burned with the same splendid prodigality; the rocking-chairs faced each other as of old, and even the accustomed stocking was rolled up on the bracket. He stood for a moment warming himself at the blaze, and watching the door for the entrance of the mistress of the house, recalling with an almost painful precision the sense of anxiety and desolation with which he had watched and waited before. But, after all, it had been the threshold of a new and better life; it had given him the friend whose strength had buttressed his weakness, and whose love had taught unselfishness to his own.

Perhaps there was not much more cordiality in Mrs. Cartwright's greeting on this occasion than on the former one, of which his mind was full; for whatever else had softened, it was not her distrust and jealousy of Gilbert Yorke.

He had come not to see her, of course, but her

son, and she told him without any compunction that John was absent from home—had been so for some days on official business—and that, therefore, his object would be lost.

'But my uncle—of course I called in to see him as I passed—told me that he was expected home to-day. I am come to throw myself on your hospitality—to ask you to let me occupy my old room to-night, and not to begrudge Jack and me a talk over the fire.'

His manner and smile were delightful, but Mrs. Cartwright had always succeeded in hardening her heart against the charm.

'John will be very tired,' was her answer. 'He is overtasked with work and responsibility of all kinds, and whenever you seek him it is to make a demand of some kind or another. However,' with a reluctant smile, 'I can scarcely refuse your request.'

And so it happened that towards midnight the cousins found themselves together in the familiar "spare room," a generous fire blazing in the grate, and the historical chair wheeled within its range. Gilbert had insisted, as in their boyish days, upon John occupying it, while he himself stood restlessly leaning against the high mantel or taking a tour of inspection through the room. They had heard the doors of the house closed and bolted one after the other, and now the silence and solitude reigned for which Gilbert's soul had longed. He had turned out the gas jet, which filled the room with light, so that there was now no other illumination than that supplied by the cheerful flames of the fire.

John sat taciturn, as was often his habit, and that he was tired and overtasked was evidently no figment of maternal anxiety; but there was not any sullenness in his silence. The mind of each was heavy and depressed, but none the less the old magnetic *rapport* was felt between them. Gilbert broke the silence by saying :

'You do not ask me what has brought me here to-day. It would make it easier if you would.'

'I do not ask because I thought I understood. You wish to know more than my letter told you.' And as John answered he lifted up his eyes, heavy with sleepless nights and days of torment, for on his impassioned and tenacious spirit the yoke of renunciation still pressed sorely.

'Scarcely that!' said Gilbert sharply. 'I have news to give you—my engagement is broken off— at least, my cousin writes to tell me that I am a free man.'

John neither spoke nor moved. Inwardly he flinched under the announcement as if a blow had struck him, while at the same time he condemned himself for doing so. Could any event separate him farther from Margery than he had separated himself? And if so, why did he shrink as if hot iron had touched his flesh at the news which made it possible that the man for whose sake mainly he had resisted his temptation might make his profit of the sacrifice?

'Tell me about it,' he said in a low, stifled voice. 'It was not your doing?'

'Indirectly it was my doing.' And Gilbert explained that Philippa based her resolution on the discovery of the copy of his own letter.

John asked: 'Have you decided to take her at her word?'

'That would scarcely be the course that honour would exact! I go up to-morrow to see my cousin —to give what explanations I can, and to try and reconcile her to carry out our engagement. My aunt will not fail to help me.'

'You mean that you are anxious to effect a reconciliation?' There was a feverish eagerness in John's mind for which he hated himself, and which communicated itself to his voice.

Gilbert looked at him in surprise. 'What is wrong between us?' he asked. 'Are you suspecting me of the baseness of turning this to any account against you? If I find I can take my freedom honourably, I will take it and thank God, but it cannot make a hair's breadth of difference to the position in which you stand to Miss Denison.'

He stopped, but the other did not answer.

'In that case,' he resumed, 'I should shut up Rookhurst for the short tenure that will be left to me, and go—well, further afield than I have yet been. My plans are scarcely fixed. I shall not come back, Jack, till I am sure of myself, and am able to witness the happiness that I still find it hard to wish you. Do you ask more of poor human nature than this?'

'I do not ask so much. What need of more words? You have had my letter—have I failed to make you understand that there is nothing between us?'

'But there will be! You cannot stand by your denial and make her miserable in vain—what profit is there in such a sacrifice? It is to say this as much as the other that I am come. The best turn you can do me, Jack, is to make her happy for whom I would lay down my life.'

To this, again, there was no immediate reply. John Cartwright's figure seemed to shrink still further into the depths of the chair in which he sat, with his elbow on its arm, and his chin propped on his hand, so that the firelight fell full upon his face. Its aspect was at once stern and haggard, the dark eyes glowing like live coals in the midst of its dark pallor. As Gilbert spoke, a momentary spasm contracted his features; it was as if all the kingdoms of the world and the glory of them had been set before him by the Tempter, and that he lacked the courage to cry, *Retro me Sathana!* Then, suddenly he stretched out his hand and grasped Gilbert's.

'Let us leave all this,' he said, in a husky voice; 'I cannot trust myself to-night—nor in the morning either. Go and see your cousin as you propose, and I will meet you at Rookhurst when you come back. For the rest, there never was a time since I knew you when you did not set me lessons hard to learn.'

He got up without waiting for an answer, and went out to his own room.

The reception given by Mrs. Yorke to her nephew was one of condemnation held in discreet reserve. The fact that he had come at all mollified her, and she did not wish to alienate his good will. As he arrived late, Gilbert saw no one but his aunt, Philippa having gone to her room, and Edward, of course, never assuming the duties of a host. Mrs. Yorke suggested that there should be no discussion of the matter that had brought him until the morning, but the young man's anxiety was such that he could not help questioning her about Philippa's state of feeling, and the chances of a reconciliation.

'On that point,' said Mrs. Yorke austerely, 'she herself is the only one that can inform you. I can only say that she feels very strongly. I do not think I should have induced her to explain the circumstance that had led her to act as she has done, but unfortunately her brother was acquainted with the facts, or, rather, he has been her informant and instigator throughout. You will not wonder he has no love for you, and even he could detect and resent your indifference to his sister.'

'An indifference of which I had made no secret to her mother!' rejoined Gilbert with flashing eyes. 'To my mind it had appeared an obstacle not to be overcome, but she judged otherwise.'

'I grant it,' said Mrs. Yorke quietly. 'My daughter's regard for you and the family conditions justified me in the course I adopted. We all know what a young man's first love is worth; it was as much for your own sake as for hers that I declined to sacrifice substance to shadow.' Then, with contemptuous bitterness, she added: 'What is to be said of the discretion, even the honour, of a man who throws about, to be picked up by servants, such damaging evidence of his folly as you have done? My son's valet brought the precious effusion to his master, and the brother communicated with the sister. The child wrote to you in the first heat of wounded feeling without even consulting me.'

'Such conduct was in every way worthy of my cousin Edward,' replied Gilbert, with a calmness that gave the greater effect to his words. 'I am sorry that I have made Philippa unhappy, but I am glad that she knows the truth—that is, if we are to become man and wife.'

Mrs. Yorke softened. 'It is still your wish and intention to try and persuade her to this?'

'It is my intention,' he said, flushing deeply. 'I have never deceived you as to the direction in which my wishes lie.' And at this point Mrs. Yorke thought it best to close the conversation, and dismiss her nephew to his room.

But the next day brought unexpected complications. Philippa positively refused to grant Gilbert Yorke an interview, and Edward shrilly and eagerly backed her resolution. He was quite as afraid as his sister that her steadfastness might not be proof against her cousin's solicitations, and the dread of

being disappointed in respect to Gilbert's forfeiture
of the inheritance transported him to the verge of
madness. Even the wary and dispassionate Mrs.
Yorke lost her patience under these provocations;
she reproached her son bitterly for his share in
bringing about the present state of things, and
tried—what had never been known to fail before
—the direct exercise of her authority over her
daughter. But though Philippa wept, she was
firm.

'This once,' she said, 'you must let me have
my own way. My mind is quite made up. If he
were to beg me on his knees I would refuse, knowing
his motive. I would refuse, mother, if you were
to turn me out of doors for refusing! I would die
rather than marry him!'

Her pale cheeks flamed, and her beautiful gray
eyes were distended with passion and pain. She
had never looked so handsome in her life, and Mrs.
Yorke sighed, wishing that Gilbert could have seen
her.

'Why have you brought him here?' pursued the girl, in a strained, unnatural voice. 'Send him away, mother, if—if you have any love or pity left. The thought of *his* pity almost kills me!'

Mrs. Yorke recognised reluctantly that nothing was to be done with her—at present, at any rate. Her own mind was greatly exasperated; she resented almost equally Gilbert's carelessness, Fletcher's dishonest meddling, and Edward's selfish action. The anguish of poor Philippa softened her heart towards her.

From Philippa she went to her son's room, drawn thither by the sound of his voice in shrill, excited outburst, and before entering she paused at the door to listen. Accustomed as she was to the coarse violence of his language under provocation, she was yet startled and distressed at some of the phrases that assailed her ears, and at the pitch of excitement he seemed to have reached. It was evident that Gilbert was with him, and that he was pouring out on his head the foul vials of his wrath and hate without restraint of any sort.

Mrs. Yorke opened the door with a trembling hand, her fear being lest the object of such insult should turn upon his assailant and chastise him.

But her first glance at Gilbert showed her she had no ground for apprehension, although the sight of him stabbed her heart with a new pang almost more keen than that which it had superseded. It was not so much the young man's handsome face and figure which the contrast offered by her unhappy son threw into strong relief, but it was the aspect of moral dignity—the sort of compassionate aloofness with which he stood regarding the inflamed and distorted countenance of his cousin.

'Enough of this,' he said at last, for she had entered so quietly that neither heard her. 'A mind like yours makes its hell in advance. If you had not hated me I must have been hateful.'

Edward's answer was a snarl of baffled rage, for the words, with their bell-like distinctness of utterance and the absence of all passion in the speaker, drove him to frenzy. He was on the point of another outbreak, when Mrs. Yorke stepped forward and announced herself.

'I think,' she said, facing her nephew with an effort, 'that it will be well, Gilbert, for you to leave the room. Our poor Edward is scarcely responsible for this violence of temper. It is a sort of hysteria beyond moral control. Also as a brother his provocation has been very·great. Shall we agree to say farewell? Your presence troubles us all.'

'That is just as you please. I am willing to wait longer in the hope that Philippa may consent to see me, or to go at once, if you think that best.'

'I think it best that you should go. The matter is finished.'

She had led the way out of Edward's room, and had paused, as on a former occasion, to speak a few last words in the hall.

'This matter is finished,' she repeated, 'and it may be that I have been the most to blame. I bear you no malice, Gilbert.'

'But you do not disown me,' he said, with real anxiety, and taking her hand affectionately. 'Remember that—I have no mother !'

'And I no son, you might say.'

Her lip trembled. Gilbert put the hand he held to his lips with a quiet sympathy that softened her more than words. Her eyes were full of tears when she spoke again.

'At least, let it be understood that we do not part in anger. If Philippa should come to a better mind——' She hesitated, seeing the colour rush into his face, and added : 'But no, that would not be fair to you. I have already said—the matter is finished.'

'I am going abroad,' said Gilbert, 'for a year or

two, but I will wait at Rookhurst for one month from now to hear from you. If Philippa sends for me within that time I will come.'

And on this understanding they parted.

CHAPTER XXIV.

A MIDNIGHT REVELATION.

IT had cost John Cartwright a struggle of desperate severity, calling into play all the resources of his strength, before he had accepted the necessity of renunciation. Gilbert Yorke, after a moment's pause of hesitation, had consented to risk anew the freedom to which he clung with passionate desire, moved by the tears in a woman's eyes.

The month that Gilbert Yorke spent at Rookhurst brought with it new and deeper experiences. He had gone to see John and to Fair Lawns against the advice of his physician, because it had seemed to him a point of honour to do so. The consequence was that he had so increased the mischief in his knee that absolute rest had become a matter not of precaution, but of necessity. Through the long winter days, brightened chiefly by the assiduities of his attached servants and the visits of his medical attendant, Gilbert had plenty of time to review the past and forecast the future. The influence of his ancestral surroundings and the memory of his grandfather made themselves felt with a strength they had never seemed to possess before. Now that he had absolutely relinquished the hopes that had made life beautiful, he began to ask himself what better course was open to him than to fulfil the destiny appointed him by Sir Owen Yorke? Undoubtedly he owed to him a heavy debt of gratitude, for, whatever his shortcomings and transgressions towards others had been, the worldly old man had loaded his grandson with benefits. Was he justified in thrusting from him the responsibilities which had been so deliberately imposed?

The thought of his father stricken down in early manhood, an alien from his birthright, and the adored mother who had so passionately deplored the ruin which the love of her had brought with it, quickened the growing sense. His own restoration to the family honours would have been balm and healing to those wounds which had bled till death. Besides, in a life bereft of the blessedness he had sought, it was necessary to put something in its place if moral and mental collapse were to be avoided—something that would brace and fortify the spirit better than abandonment to an adored art, and what more powerful than duty ?

The duty of administering a large property wisely and well; the duty of cherishing and encouraging the gentle girl who loved him ; the duty of giving practical proof that his friend's gain should not prove his own irremediable loss. To this mind Gilbert Yorke brought himself not easily or at once, but by the slow illuminating process of self-judgment used in solitude. There was also a subtle reflex influence from long association with John Cartwright : words that he had spoken, still more the silent acts which are so much more potent than words—the tune, as it were, to which he had set his life—stimulated and confirmed Gilbert's nobler purpose.

So, when at last the expected letter from Fair Lawns came into his hands, though his face whitened and his heart beat quicker, his resolution to face the situation and to respond loyally to the expected summons never faltered for a moment.

But it is the experience of life that events seem to mock our prescience. We tax endurance to meet the misfortune that never happens, and smile incredulously at the idea of another which overwhelms us unawares. Loins are girded and sinews braced for the conflict, when the fiat comes that our strength is to sit still; while the veteran, reposing after the heat and labour of the day, hears the sudden call to arms, and springs erect to buckle on the armour scarcely laid aside.

And, again, there are those amongst us whom the gods love, for whom the valleys are exalted and the rough places made plain, and to this category Gilbert Yorke belonged.

He had nerved himself to the double duty of accepting his inheritance and of marrying his cousin not because the one depended on the other, but because she loved him; and the sacrifice of self which had seemed so costly to the young man as he had bound it to the altar, was given back to him unscathed.

Mrs. Yorke wrote to repeat what she had said before—'the matter is finished.' Philippa adhered to her resolution with a firmness not to be shaken by any consideration which her mother could put before her. She sent her love and best wishes to her cousin Gilbert, and with these gifts she sent the assurance that he was absolutely free, and might make use of his freedom without self-reproach or blame from her. In proof of goodwill he was to come and see them at Fair Lawns as soon as he returned from his travels.

Gilbert read the letter twice through. As he

put it down the slanting rays of the setting sun poured a pale opalescent glory over the wide prospect of park and garden, pasture and snow-tipped hills, which his window afforded. Far as his eye could reach, and farther still beyond his vision, he was master of all, and not of these only, but also of the splendid appanage of the Holywell estates—until the hour should strike which completed the year of probation fixed by the will of Sir Owen Yorke.

To say he felt no regret as this thought passed through his mind would be to say that Gilbert Yorke was stock or stone, but certain it is that after this first instinctive pang of recognition he felt the deprivation as little as it was possible for a young man to do.

The means left him would be enough for his wants. The joy of travel was before him, and the stern duty of forgetting the wife of his friend—for that John would ultimately overcome his generous scruples and marry Margery, Gilbert felt assured.

As for the joys of life—his violin leaned against the corner of the wall, and the wide world of musical art was his to enter in and to possess it.

John Cartwright had not gone to Rookhurst as had been proposed.   He had been sent into Cornwall by the heads of his Church, charged with a mission of inspection over a large outlying district which had broken loose from the bonds in which it had been held by the Connexion ever since the days of Wesley and Whitfield.   The season was inclement, and the duties somewhat severe, but John had embraced the commission with avidity.

Love and sorrow were still at strife within him, defying the authority with which he ordered them to submission.   The sight of Margery Denison in her pew at Castle Street Chapel produced a suffocating conflict which left the victor wan and exhausted, and drew upon him—not, as before, his mother's urgent questioning, but what was still harder to bear—the reproach of her silence and watchful tenderness.   It would be well, therefore, to embrace the opportunity of escape; absence might—*should* help him.

The night before his departure an incident occurred which was to change the current of his life. He had gone to bed late, as was becoming a habit with him, for he had been striving to set heart and life in order before he entered upon his appointed service. There was no infirmity of purpose, nor any desire to draw back from the position he had taken; yet he held that victory was not achieved until inclination and will should be at one together —until he could be *content* to forego that which he had resolved should be foregone. Moreover, it was necessary for a man pledged as he was to the divine race to lay aside absolutely the clogs and hindrances of earthly passion and regret, not to rest in the mere recognition of them as such. ' This woman I have loved,' he said to himself, ' but I will never love again. I will take the pain and the loss as experience that may help me to feel for others.'

He went to bed at last and slept soundly for an hour or two ; then he awoke with a sudden curious consciousness that he was not alone, and, as he held his breath and lay quite still to verify the impression, he became aware that his mother was kneeling by his bedside.

He had the habit of drawing up his blind the last thing at night, and the moon, now at the full, was riding high over the house-tops in the cold, cloudless wintry heavens — clearer than at any other hour in the twenty-four—and flooding the room with light.

The light fell on the face of the kneeling figure, raised in an ecstasy of supplication, and the beauty and spiritual elevation of that face, familiar from infancy as it was, struck upon the son's sense with a new force.

The white woollen wrapper that she wore, and the loosened masses of her magnificent hair, gave to it an aspect of softness and relaxation which touched those deep springs of tenderness that had been too often checked by her habitual air of sternness and repression.

John instantly perceived, first, that she supposed him to be asleep, and then that self-consciousness was lost in exaltation of feeling. He shrank almost equally from his involuntary trespass upon her communion with God and from the painful duty of warning her that he was awake; and while he deliberated her prayer became vocal, and compelled him to silence:

' I acknowledge my sin,' was her cry, ' the sin of blindness and self-will, but visit me not in judgment! I am unworthy of what Thy goodness hath vouchsafed, but the thing which my soul longs for is still denied. Give me, O God, the heart that I have hardened against me, and the grace to find favour with my son!'

She stopped, for a sob choked her, then resumed:

' Break down the barrier that I have built up—chasten me as Thou wilt, if only the life of my life is strengthened and consoled!'

John could contain himself no longer—he sprang up, calling upon her name with a sudden passionate cry, and holding out his arms to embrace her.

For one moment the pride of years and the sharp pain of a reserved spirit wounded where it is most sensitive, bound the flow of Rachel Cartwright's feelings, but the next her son's dark head was on her bosom, his lips against her cheek, and each was clasped in the other's arms so closely that heart beat against heart.

Let us drop the curtain over that sacred hour of union, where the mother poured out her confession at the feet of the son, and the son took half the burden of the passionate blame upon himself, and forgave as he hoped to be forgiven. When the first strong emotions had subsided, John put the seal upon their reconciliation by the disclosure of his love for Margery Denison ; he kept nothing back, though such new confidence was difficult, and a thousand manly shames and tender scruples urged their plea of secrecy.

But his mother sat on the side of his bed, her hand clasped in his and her tender eyes following his half-reluctant story with a sympathy so prompt and intimate as to give to him the courage he had lacked at first, and to her the first draught of that power of consolation for which she had prayed.

When she was quite sure he had told all, she said in a low voice of exquisite gentleness :

' Do not let us deceive ourselves at the beginning ! I understand you to mean that it is not for my sake that you give up Margery Denison—that if no exacting mother existed you would still do the same ?'

' Yes, that is right. I give her up for her own sake, and for mine, as I have explained ; and, still more, I give her up for the sake of Gilbert Yorke.'

It was indicative of a radical change of mood and mind that Mrs. Cartwright heard these words and made no protest. For a few minutes longer she sat silent with her eyes on the ground ; the moon was setting, and it was difficult to distinguish her face. Then she said :

'It was a proof of her own worth that she loved you, John, but I think you have done right. She is generous and very winning, but there is too much of worldly alloy in her nature to fit her to fight the fight to which you are pledged and not to count the cost. If only it may be given me to do my poor part to make up for what you lose ! You will not shut your heart against me—ever again ?'

'Never, so help me God ! I am consoled already.'

He pressed her closer.

'You will take cold. My father will wake up and be frightened. You must promise on your side to submit to my authority. . . . I must send you away !'

She lingered a little longer, then rose to go, stooping to kiss him before she went.

John caught her hands and pressed them passionately to his lips.

' I feel like a child again,' he said, ' and yet as a child I was never so happy as now. It is not a dream, mother ?'

' No,' she answered, with a smile more pathetic than tears, ' it is not a dream. . . . We are awake now for the first time in our lives.'

*   *   *   *   *

John returned from his journey fortified and refreshed. The keen pure air, the exhilarating ocean, the utter change of scene and character, the practical exercise of the religion to which he was devoted, and, more than all, the life-giving remembrance of his mother as she had last disclosed herself, which abode with him night and day, invigorated and warmed his heart. He became able to recall the idea of Margery without shrinking as from a touch of torture, and to forecast her future as Gilbert's wife in the temper of a noble acquiescence rather than of voluntary martyrdom.

On his return after a month's absence, he felt an acute anxiety as to the manner in which his mother would receive him—lest any of that distance and coldness which had marred their lives hitherto should have crept again between them. But the first moment of meeting dispelled the apprehension ; the light in her eyes, the smile on her lips, the tones of her voice, told him that not only was all that he wanted waiting for his acceptance, but that there remained depths of comprehension and tenderness which to fathom might be the business of his lifetime and to exhaust was impossible.

Martin Cartwright, genial and cheerful as was his wont, received from the new sweetness and serenity in his wife an impression that he scarcely understood and made no attempt to analyze. He basked in the deeper peace and happiness of his home as unconsciously as a cat in the sunshine. It delighted the good man's heart that his eyes could rest upon his son in his accustomed place again and looking so much better for the change.

'There were those who thought the work and the climate at such a season as this would have been too much for you, John,' he said; 'but, to my mind, hard work always agrees with the best amongst us—eh, mother?'

The mother and son exchanged looks of loving intelligence, and Martin Cartwright, who was brimful of local gossip and not quite so much interested as his wife in the report of the Cornish miners, poured forth the flood upon John's head as they sat at supper.

'I wanted to write to thee, lad, but th' mother objected. "Good news," she said, "can always wait, and it would be a pity to divert your mind from the work." But you shall have it now! I suppose that news must be good which helps the fortunes of Gilbert Yorke? Eh, but he's a lucky dog!'

And with this preamble he went on to explain in detail what we will sum up in a few words.

The information given was in respect to Sir Owen Yorke's will, and the informant had been no less an authority than the old lawyer, Mr.

Percival himself, who was also the solicitor habitually consulted by Martin Cartwright. A matter of business had brought them recently together, and it was natural enough that the conversation should drift to the affairs of Gilbert Yorke and his position as it now stood under his grandfather's will.

All the county had known the terms of the will, and had been equally informed of the engagement between the cousins and of the speedy rupture that had followed. The announcement of the latter fact had been very explicitly made in the newspapers, and was qualified by the statement that it was entirely due to the action of the lady, quite independent of any personal considerations touching the young man's integrity and honour. Mr. Percival informed his client that this paragraph had been inspired by himself after consultation with Miss Yorke. He had been summoned to Fair Lawns by her mother in the hope that he might be able to bring the young lady to another mind, but he found her obdurate, and had thereupon been obliged to act upon the necessity of making her determination to reject her cousin as public and unmistakable as the announcement of their engagement.

'It appears not to have been generally understood,' the lawyer had added, 'that Gilbert Yorke inherits under his grandfather's will if he is prepared to fulfil his part of the contract, the lady's obstinacy notwithstanding. The clause in the will is intentionally obscure according to the design of the testator, and its meaning seems to have been missed by every member of the family. Even the young man himself does not appear to be aware of it, but has taken himself off to the ends of the earth.'

'I do not believe,' said John, as Martin Cartwright brought his story to a close, 'that Gilbert ever took the trouble to read his grandfather's will. Mr. Percival sent him a statement of its conditions when he was ill in Vienna, from which this saving clause was entirely excluded, and he accepted it implicitly without any attempt at verification.'

'But you are pleased, John?' questioned his father.

'More than pleased. I rejoice with all my heart.' He looked towards his mother and smiled. 'It will make things easier for Gilbert.'

It appeared to him precisely such a benefaction as his friend's disinterestedness deserved—one which he would himself have delighted to bestow had the power been his.

He cast over the matter anxiously in his mind as he sat over his bedroom fire.

When Gilbert returned sooner or later from his travels, still true to the love of his youth, what more inevitable than that Margery should yield at length to the power of this fidelity when the great obstacle which had stood between them was removed?

As for her feeling towards himself, it still appeared to him one of those problems presented by the inexplicable mystery of a woman's nature. Knight errantry was not confined to the one sex.

She loved him (or thought that she did) because he had saved her life; because few loved him and society at large held him to be unlovable and obscure; or because in her moments of spiritual concern for herself or others she had found help and comfort in his words; or, again, because the friend, dear to him as his own soul, had made her think him to be something very different from what he really was.

Whereas Gilbert himself . . . here the thinker paused with a smile of tender reminiscence which yet had a dash of self-mockery in it:

'Let her only take his friend at the value he himself put upon him, and there would be nothing left for even a lover to desire.'

CHAPTER XXV.

THE DIVIDING OF THE WAYS.

A DAY or two after John's return Mrs. Cartwright received an unexpected visit from Margery Denison. Such calls had frequently been made before, but some months had now elapsed since the two women had met. Mrs. Cartwright was alone, for the men of her household were both engaged in their respective callings, and, while thankful that this was so, she felt a complex embarrassment at the prospect of the interview.

The maid had shown the visitor into the drawing-room, a stiff, comfortless apartment seldom used by the family, and where on this occasion no fire was burning, so that the hostess went at once to fetch

Margery into the cheerful warmth of the familiar dining parlour, and with her somewhat formal and old-fashioned courtesy not only placed her in her own easy-chair, but brought a cushion for her feet.

'Loosen your furs, my dear,' she said, 'or you will find no benefit from them when you go out;' and as she spoke she offered her own services with a softness of voice and manner that struck the keen perceptions of the girl as significant.

In truth, as Mrs. Cartwright looked at her and recognised not only the beauty that distinguished her, but the enchanting grace of expression, voice and gesture, she was conscious of a momentary sense of triumph that such a woman should love her son, and of doubt whether it were absolutely necessary that such a love should be put aside on the grounds of duty or of friendship. She comprehended the difficulty of her son's renunciation as she had never done before, and asked herself with a sharp anxiety whether it would indeed be in her own power to make amends and to console.

Margery caught the hand that was busy with the fastenings of her cloak.

'What has happened?' she demanded, in her direct and slightly imperious way. 'There is a different look in your eyes and a new tone in your voice. Ah, I see! You know our secret.'

Our secret! Rachel Cartwright winced a little, then conquered the weakness.

'Yes,' she said, in a tone full of sensibility . . . 'for it is better to be honest—I know it. It satisfies my pride that you should love my son, and warms my heart towards you; bear with me if I say that you do yourself as much honour as him.'

Margery continued to sit looking up into the speaker's face with the intense clear gaze her blue eyes had retained from her childhood, while a half smile of mockery touched her lips. It seemed as if she were bent on reading the secrets of the mother's heart.

'Will you give him to me, then?' she asked, in a voice so charged with passionate feeling that it startled Mrs. Cartwright. Was it with such an accent that she had spoken to her son and he had been strong enough to resist?

'My dear,' was her answer, 'I would give him what is best for him at any cost of personal feeling, but I would refuse him his heart's desire if I thought it put his soul in peril.'

'But why should it do that?' asked Margery. 'If he has made you his confidante, he has told you that I am willing to give up the pomps and vanities of this wicked world and to take up the service to which he is pledged—in a word, to follow where he leads. I would prove to you that Margery Denison could make as good a wife for a Wesleyan minister, who has the devotion of a saint with the humility of a child, as any shallow pious girl you might choose for him out of his congregation.' Her eyes flashed. 'I at least am able to understand what I love, and have enough experience of other men to gauge John Cartwright's difference! I was even willing to conform myself to the jealousy of your affection.'

'And you would have made shipwreck of his life and of your own!' returned the other in a tone of subdued but intense conviction. 'I know that you are a noble woman, and I estimate every grace and gift which makes you one amongst a thousand, so that I marvel where my son found the courage to address or the strength to resist you. And yet I marvel not! But I am bound to tell you that the purpose to lead the divine life which is not founded on the love of God, and on the humility that comes of deep conviction of sin, is like the house that was built upon the sand. You would soon have flagged in a race that taxes hard the endurance even of the faithful soldiers of our Lord. I see it all so plainly! Weariness and impatience would have followed when you watched the unabated zeal with which he pursued objects which had become flat and tiresome to you. You could not help begrudging his devotion, and you would have tried to wean his heart from God in order that he might love you more.'

'And you have told him this and strengthened his purpose? Was it your doing that he went away?'

'I have spoken no word of all this, and his purpose needed no strengthening. He loved you too well to risk the chance of your disappointment. My dear,' she added, with extreme gentleness, resting her hands lightly on the girl's shoulders and looking into the proud downcast face, 'you would surely have been disappointed! Our ways are not as your ways, and many a natural instinct and innocent desire would have cried out for indulgence and met no response.'

Margery rose from her seat and looked steadily at her companion, though she lifted her eyes with a sort of reluctance. As the two women stood thus it appeared that they were both of the same height, and that the beauty and dignity of each were almost equal, except that the one had the splendid advantage of the bloom of youth.

'I ask you again,' said Margery, 'what has

happened? You look and speak unlike yourself! I know that you have always loved your son, but —let it appear! Has this—this trouble of ours, for I know that he has suffered, brought you two closer together? If so, I am glad.'

It was not possible for Mrs. Cartwright to belie the reticence of her nature. She contented herself with a gesture of assent, and the colour rose in her face.

Margery continued to watch her, then suddenly turned aside and began to refasten her cloak.

'I think,' she said, 'I shall be able to trust you to be good to him, and I am glad that you know.' She paused, for her heart was sore, and she did not wish her voice to betray her. 'I did not come here,' she continued, with a gleam of pathetic humour lighting up her face, 'to engage your good offices with your son. If I had, I see I should have failed, but I had taken my dismissal before. I am not of the sort to do otherwise. Do you not wonder why I came to see the mother of the man who had refused me?'

'It was gracious and sweet of you to come, whatever might be your object.'

'My object was to bid you good-bye, and to give you a message for Mr. Cartwright. I might have put it differently had you not known, and spoken as you have done ; but now the same words I have just used will serve for him. Tell him—I accept my dismissal. He has nothing to fear from me.'

'My dear, do not speak like that! You fill me with distress and shame. My son will love you to the last hour of his life. He is not one of those who let go.'

Margery drew a deep breath. 'And perhaps I am! I do not know. Anyway, my dream of being a good woman is over—bear that on your conscience when you pray !'

'I have no fears,' said Mrs. Cartwright tenderly. 'You will make some other life noble.'

Margery smiled a little bitterly. 'What will be will be,' she answered. 'Meantime, my aunt and I start for the Riviera to-morrow. Her health

requires the warm sunshine, and so does mine.
We are going to Monaco. I thought it right that
you should know.'

She stopped rather suddenly, and Mrs. Cartwright asked :

' But you are surely coming back again ?'

' Oh yes, after some time. My aunt likes The
Hollies, and looks upon it as home; but we may
travel for a year. We have been stay-at-homes
so long.'

' May we ever hope to hear from you ?'

' I think not ; I am a poor letter-writer, but you
will know, of course, when we are coming back.
We leave a trustworthy caretaker, but we shall
like to feel that our landlord also will safeguard
our house. And now farewell !'

She held out her hand.

' Do not detain me ! I want no escort,' she
added, in reply to some suggestion from the other.
' My pony-carriage is at the hotel, and I can walk
back there quite as well as I came.'

Mrs. Cartwright looked at her with softened eyes.

'May I kiss you?' she asked, almost timidly. 'I feel as if we were treating a generous benefactor with base ingratitude.'

'I think so, too,' returned the girl, with a smile half sad, half humorous; 'but I forgive you! You both followed your conscience, and I have remarked that this habit leaves little room for loving-kindness or tender mercy.'

She allowed her hostess to kiss her, but she did not return the salute.

'I will go now,' she said. 'Do not come with me to the door, or ring for a servant, but we will part friends. I wish well to all who sleep or wake under this roof to-night.'

Her fortitude was to be put to a further strain that morning. As she walked towards the town she saw John Cartwright approaching from the opposite direction, so that a meeting was unavoidable. Such was her frame of mind that she would gladly have escaped it had it been possible, but as it was not she accepted the inevitable.

As they neared each other John glanced towards her with deep anxiety, as if wishing to guide his conduct according to her initiative. Margery, with her keen vision, saw that he had flushed and paled at the sight of her; but she saw too with equal distinctness that his eyes had lost the strained look of secret trouble which they had worn when they last met and parted.

The colour rose into her own cheek, and a throb of indignation made her eyes flash, and gave an added dignity to the poise of her figure.

Her thought was: 'How soon these good men reconcile themselves to their duty!'

When they were within a few paces of each other the young man raised his hat with a bow so deep as to be almost reverential, and which served to quicken the irritation of Margery's excited mood. She would have passed with a courteous but stately inclination of the head, had not John forestalled her intention by speaking.

' You are alone. May I be permitted to see you safely wherever you may be going ?'

For a moment Margery gazed at him steadily, in defiance of her secret weakness, as if to impress upon her memory the characteristics of person and manner which she knew so well. In that face there was no beauty to attract, nor in his address was there any special grace or sweetness to allure, and yet she shrank, though not outwardly, from his modest yet direct gaze, and from the tones of his voice. ' That is as you please,' she said, with that fine air of distance and reserve which recalled the impression of the early years before she had shown herself gracious to him. ' I am going to the hotel where my servant and carriage are in waiting, but if it appears to you to be your duty to see me to the door, which is in view, I do not object, especially as it will give me the opportunity of telling you what I have already told your mother—that we are going away.'

She saw he bore the intelligence without wincing; not from lack of feeling, but because John Cartwright had forecast every contingency in past hours of suffering, and was therefore armed at all points.

'Do you mean that you have been so good as to visit my mother?' he asked in a very low tone, for he was half afraid to trust himself to speak.

'Yes, we are going to Monaco first, and then shall travel for some months—a year, perhaps, so I have been paying farewell visits to all my friends. Your mother has been very kind to me——' She stopped, raised her head, and added firmly: 'So also has her son. I do not forget anything when I say this. I wish to part friends, Mr. Cartwright. Is there any law against that?'

They had reached the inn-door. She held out her hand as if to dismiss him without the option of reply. Moreover, it was market-day in Copple-stone, and the entrance was besieged with comers and goers, so that an answer other than the most conventional would have been impossible. But Margery saw that John had no words to answer, even if they had stood alone in some primæval solitude.

CHAPTER XXVI.

AN ARTIST'S TRIUMPH.

THE next twelve months, which passed with all the swiftness of an ordered monotony to the Cartwright household, passed scarcely more swiftly to Gilbert Yorke, who spent the same period in more or less adventurous travel, and whose letters to his friend were as frequent as circumstances would allow, and as loyal as John's heart could desire.

But travel and adventure were not as the breath of life to this young man, as to so many of his countrymen, and in the second year of his exile he began to yearn for home and intimate fellowship, for the opera-houses and chamber music of Europe, and, above all, for those possibilities which he knew circumstances had not yet put out of his reach. No man was ever a more faithful lover— so far as he had been able to ascertain Margery was still unmarried—and John, on the one occasion when her name was mentioned in his letters, had assured him that no possibility of union subsisted between them. Hence Gilbert Yorke was free to repeat the question asked and answered so often before.

At Suez Gilbert found letters that had been awaiting him for months, and which served still further to hasten his return. Mr. Percival wrote to inform him of the death of his cousin Edward Yorke, not from his congenital weakness, but from a sudden attack of lung disease, and the old lawye advised Gilbert's immediate return home to look after his affairs, and to live the life of an English country gentleman.

'Rookhurst and Holywells are still yours,' he wrote, 'though you seem to have turned your back on your good fortune. If you have any doubt of my meaning, five minutes' conference in my chambers will remove it.' A letter from John of a more recent date elucidated Mr. Percival's, and it also told him that the ladies of The Hollies had written to his father to announce their return within a few weeks, and that their letter had been dated from Florence.

Thither Gilbert went, a new hope feeding the undying flame of his love. Besides, a visit to Florence was always an act of religion with him.

There were his mother's grave and his most sacred memories; there were still to be found the English chaplain who had befriended him and the *maestro*, as he still called him, who had discovered and trained his musical faculty. On this occasion a curious thing happened.

On going to the old man's house he found him in a state of great agitation and distress in consequence of a disabling accident which he had just encountered.

In making his chocolate that morning—a duty

he never suffered the old woman who waited upon him to perform—he had scalded his left hand so severely that it would be impossible for him to fulfil his professional engagements. He was first violin at the Teatro Goldini, and the opera of *Fidelio* was to be given on the following night. The difficulty that threw him into a fever of anxiety was where, at such short notice, should he be able to find a substitute.

Gilbert, with a blush almost as deep and a humility almost as deferential as when he had been a boy, proffered his own services, should the master think them available. He was intimately acquainted with the score; he had studied at Leipzig and elsewhere almost ever since he had left Florence, and there were still twenty-four hours for practice !

The old musician seized the offer with avidity; it delivered him from the rankling apprehension lest the man who stood below him, and who was already a formidable rival, should step into his

place and maintain the position, and he had also a
warm recollection of the talent he had fostered.

Gilbert had not thought it necessary to go into
careful particulars about his altered fortunes, and
his old friend regarded him with much the same
patronizing kindness as when he had given him
lessons in return for humble duties fulfilled.   He
found the young man very handsome and charming, but that he had always been, and the consideration that now swallowed up every other was
whether he were really able to do the thing he had
ventured to propose.

Gilbert, at command, fetched his own violin,
which had been his companion in all his recent
wanderings, to Guardini's apartment, in order to
prove or perfect his fitness, though the desire had
been strong upon him to spend the day in trying
to discover whether Margery and her aunt were in
the city, and, if so, to pay his respects to them.

He put it aside, however, as a thing not to
be attempted till the present enterprise was carried

through, and which was in itself a debt of gratitude and friendship that he paid with triumphant
delight.

Guardini at the first rehearsal loaded him with
praise, expressing the most ardent approval, and
then incontinently began to correct and to advise
in respect to almost every point of treatment. To
some men aware, as Gilbert could not fail to be, of
conspicuous merit, such conduct would have been
insufferable, but he had the divine humility of the
true artist, and submitted with the docility of a
disciple.

That day and the chief part of the next were
spent in rigorous practice, and at the usual time
before the appointed hour of performance *maestro*
and pupil repaired to the theatre in an equal state
of expectation and excitement. The conductor of
the orchestra had not been informed respecting
Guardini's accident, owing to his jealous apprehension of consequences, so that there was no
alternative at the last moment but to accept the

substitute provided, and to trust kind Heaven for the result. As to that result the dress, manners, and looks of the young Englishman filled him with the most sinister misgivings. An amateur and a gentleman to boot !

The whole orchestra, animated by that *esprit de corps* never more vigorous than amongst the members of their profession, banded themselves into hard and open antagonism until Gilbert, in the half hour that he had at his disposal, won them over to a better mind with his fluent Tuscan and ready German, and by a frank narrative of the obligations he owed to il Signor Guardini.

'I shall be helpless if you will not help me,' he said as they moved to their respective places, and one and all vowed loyally to do their best.

Every true artist has his own mode of interpretation, and, happily, Gilbert's knowledge of the score was so thorough as to leave him in quiet possession of all the resources of his musical genius. He performed to admiration, and with an enthusiasm so stimulating that it communicated itself to every member of the orchestra, and spread like a wave of fire over the audience. The delighted Guardini led the *bravi* of the house, and when the close of the final movement was reached there was a unanimous call for the appearance of he young volunteer before the curtain, the facts of the case having become mysteriously known throughout the theatre.

But Gilbert had succeeded in slipping away unperceived, an impulse of modesty, and perhaps of respect to his grandfather's prejudices, making such a public exhibition of himself distasteful. Besides this, his racing pulses and exhausted energies, severely taxed during the last twenty-four hours, made the rest and seclusion of his hotel the things chiefly to be desired.

As he ran down the stairs of the theatre and stepped out on the piazza a messenger followed im, and put a letter in his hand, disappearing immediately without giving opportunity for question or waiting for reply.

The night sky was ablaze with stars and with the light of a moon that hung in the palpitating atmosphere like a golden shield; the river ran like liquid amber under its rays, and every leaf of the trees in the Boboli Gardens stood out sharply defined against the heavenly background. There would have been no difficulty in reading the smallest type, much less the bold clear handwriting of Margery Denison.

One swift comprehensive glance was enough. It ran thus:

'We are in our old quarters on the Lung' Arno; come and see us to-morrow morning. We were in the theatre, though you did not know it, and you have given us the proudest hour of our lives.'

Gilbert looked up with an expression that glorified his face—it was the rapture of an anticipated joy. For a moment he held the paper crushed against his lips, then the sound of the surging crowd behind him and the simultaneous rush of carriage or fiacre that had stood motionless the minute before told him the house was emptying, and that the solitude of the Via Romana sleeping now under the smiling night sky was a thing of the past. It was even possible he might be recognised. He called a fiacre and drove to his hotel.

CHAPTER XXVII.

SURRENDER AT DISCRETION.

THE welcome given to Sir Gilbert Yorke by Mrs. Sutherland and her niece was as gracious and cordial as even the young man could desire, but it was not more gracious or cordial than that which he had received as a boy in the same rooms years before when generosity and gratitude were the ties between them.

It almost seemed as he stood by Margery's side and looked down on the glittering river and the sauntering crowd as if Time had rolled back his record and restored to them their boyhood and girlhood, and all the light-heartedness that had gone with them.

The praises he received for his last night's work were delightful to hear when they were uttered by lips at once so dear and so discriminating as were those of Margery, whose musical culture was thorough and enlightened.

'I could scarcely describe my sensations,' she said, 'when I saw that it was you. I could not understand at first, and wondered whether nature, or art rather, had been too strong for you — stronger than wealth or rank. But the sight of poor old Guardini's swathed hand and face of intense anxiety, together with my remembrance of your former relations, explained matters, and then I had but one feeling left—the desire that you should do yourself justice. You know, I have always believed in you, but—you could not have done better, Gilbert!'

'So well,' observed Mrs. Sutherland, smiling, 'that Margery's eyes were full of tears over and over again.'

'That is quite true. There is some music that

dissolves my soul, and fills me with a sort of anguish of delight. This is especially the case with *Fidelio,* and you played with such impersonal ardour that my heart would have gone out to you as a stranger. When you ran away from the audience with that marvellous fiddle of yours under your arm, and I saw you give it a little pat and a sort of slight, sly kiss, I could resist you no longer. I scribbled the few words you got on a corner of my programme, and sent a boy in pursuit of you. It was like you to come at once.'

All this was delightful, as were the days that followed. They went over all the old ground in company, even visiting the rooms which poor Christina Yorke had occupied, and standing together by her grave. Every excursion of the old days was repeated, and others made which had not been made before; and in the evenings, which were still long, for the season was early, Margery and Gilbert practised together, trying over curious old scores of mediæval church music which Guardini had lent to his pupil.

It was all so sweet and pleasant. There was no alien influence to disturb the flow of the happy days, so that Gilbert feared to break the spell by any precipitate action on his own part, although the desire to tempt his fate once more grew daily more and more beyond his control.

Never had Margery been more enchanting or so kind, but then was not her free kindness the quality most to be deprecated by a lover?

After his habit, he wrote to John Cartwright and poured out his heart in the letter. 'And yet,' he wrote (and it was written in all sincerity) '. . . were her happiness really bound up in you and yours in her, I would even now stand aside and wish you both *bon voyage* in sincerity and truth.'

But John wrote back '. . . Their intercourse had been an episode, and it was past for both of them. He was happy in his work and in his home, with only one personal interest outside of it—his friend's return, and should he come back as the husband, actual or affianced, of Margery Denison, so much the more welcome would he be.'

Still Gilbert hesitated, and before breaking ground tried to gather encouragement or defeat from Mrs. Sutherland. He asked her boldly what she thought his chances were.

'I don't know,' was her answer; 'Margery is so difficult to understand. I have my views, to be sure, but I do not trust them as I used. Speaking as an old woman, my dear, I do not know how a young one could resist you. You are nicer than ever, and then, you see, all is come right—estates, title, and everything; but, then, Margery cares for nothing of all that! Under the rose, my dear Sir Gilbert, she has actually refused Lord Thimberley a second time. He met us in Rome in the winter, and could not rest till he had tried again. It was all in vain, though. I did my best; still I am glad now for your sake.'

But it was not till the evening before their departure for England that Gilbert summoned resolu-

tion to speak. He had come in to bid them good-bye
—he himself was going to follow in a few days—
and he found Margery sitting alone in the *loggia*,
watching the animated scene below. He stood in
silence by her side for a few minutes, looking as she
looked, and then let his eyes stray to the distant
landscape, where the setting sun was gilding the
peaks of the Apennines and steeping the pale
leaves of the olive orchards in a bath of fire.

'If I could have my wish,' he said, in the low
voice which alone seemed appropriate to the
hour and the scene, 'I would live and die in
Florence!'

Margery turned towards him with her delicate
smile.

'That would scarcely be doing your duty in that
state of life to which it has pleased God to call
you! What of the management of your great
estates—the essential seat in Parliament or on the
Justices' bench at least, to say nothing of the
duties which Sir Gilbert Yorke owes to society and

to art? What a munificent patron it will be in your power to become! Let that reconcile you to your riches. Still, my dear friend, I am inclined to believe that Fate and Sir Owen Yorke have been too kind to you. You were in your right place, the place Nature intended, when you stood with your beloved violin in your hand at the head of the Goldini orchestra. How fine you looked! If that were your vocation——'

She paused, and a flush, not caught from the sunset, passed over her face.

Gilbert knelt down quietly by her chair and took her hand.

'I understand. You mean that in that case I might have been so happy as to persuade you to cast in your lot with mine, and why not otherwise—now? I love you better than ever!'

'Because I am not worthy! I have misprized your love from the beginning—taken it as a matter of course—a boy's gift not worth a woman's acceptance. What you offer me, Gilbert, not one man in a thousand could offer, and it ought to be received by a heart as steadfast as your own. Mine, as you know, has gone astray—shall we say after a false light?—at least, after one that was very soon extinguished, and proves me therefore weak and unstable. You have too much to forgive!'

'I forgive it all. Had you taken me at my first prayer, I should have been very happy, but the happiness would have been poor and shallow in comparison with what it will be if—you take me now! Cancel all your transgressions with one word, Margery. Say you will come to me at last.'

She turned away her head and reflected with knitted brows. He waited in patience, not even pressing the hand she had not withdrawn.

'How can I come to you now,' she asked, 'and hold up my head? I refused you when you had nothing and would have stripped yourself for my sake. *Now* you offer me everything that the wise world knows no woman can refuse, and I reconsider the position and consent! It would put even such chivalry as yours to the strain!'

' But then I know, and the wise world as well, that you have refused a peerage offered more than once; therefore, if you let Lord Thimberley go and take me, it is not the accidents of position which decide your choice. Dear, let the past alone. I love you none the less that you did not love me years ago. I was not worthy. Nor that you passed me by again because John Cartwright had taken captive—was it your heart, Margery, or is that still at your own disposal ?'

She smiled.

' You have learnt to know your power and your worth, and to plead in a different style from the old times. But I am not to be taunted with impunity. If your friend gave me back my heart, sir, at least remember that Cousin Philippa would not accept yours at any price. But I do wrong to jest ! If you could have given her that, the sweet soul would have taught us new lessons in love and blessedness.'

'Do you know,' he said very quietly, 'that I have received a letter from her within the last few days, telling me how happy she and her mother are together and giving me a message for you?'

'Which you have not delivered, though your opportunities are many.'

'Yes, but my courage has not been equal to them. But I will give it you now.'

He rose as he spoke and stood before her, the flaming glory of the sunset throwing his face and figure into strong relief.

'They are very simple words, like herself. If you did not love her I would not repeat them. She says'—he looked down at the letter he had taken from his pocket—'"I want you to be happy with Margery. That is my prayer for you morning and night. If you are happy, so am I. Tell her this from me."'

He stopped, for Philippa's message touched him deeply.   Then he said :

'I have told her.   Answer, Margery!'

She sat in deep thought for some moments, then asked, looking up at him with an intense anxiety :

'Are you *sure* you love me?—*sure* that this feeling is not a shadow, a reflection, from the old real thing, or some twist or turn of chivalric feeling?   There never was so true a knight !   I don't deserve such fidelity, and am frightened lest you should be deceiving yourself.   If I became your wife and you found this out——'

They were interrupted by Mrs. Sutherland's voice calling Margery :

'My dear, you must not sit out there any longer ! You know how we have been warned of the mist that rises after sunset.'

Then perceiving her mistake, for she had thought her niece was alone, she stopped short, hesitated, and blushed like a girl.

'Oh dear, Sir Gilbert, forgive me !   I am a

blundering old woman. But I do not count anything! Am I to congratulate you?'

Each blushed and smiled, and Margery, holding out her hand to Gilbert with a shyness that
thrilled him with delight, they both stepped over
the threshold of the *loggia* into the room within.
Then she went up to her aunt and kissed her
affectionately.

'Congratulate me. Gilbert has told me once
more the old story, but I want courage to believe
that I deserve to be so happy. Speak for me, Aunt
Sutherland. His goodness makes me humble; I
am afraid of myself.'

'My dear,' was the answer, 'you know my views!
I believe you have loved Sir Gilbert Yorke all the
time without knowing it, or if not '—with a twinkle
in her eyes—'you at least fell violently in love with
him a month ago to-day at the Teatro Goldini!'

As Margery, covered with blushes, glanced towards her lover, Mrs. Sutherland slipped out of the
room.

'I believe that is true, but does it matter . . . whether then or long ago? At least, I am yours now.'

She stretched out her hand, and as he sprang to meet it and to press it against his lips and heart with a passion none the less ardent because chastened by reverence and gratitude, Margery looked down upon him as he half knelt before her with eyes full of tears.

The thought of his long fidelity, beginning as it did in the Iddersleigh meadows, touched her profoundly. She stooped lower and kissed his forehead.

'Ah,' she murmured, with her delicious smile, as she suffered him to clasp her in his arms, 'you have been faithful from a boy, but what arrears of love it will behove me to make up!'

THE END.

BILLING AND SONS, PRINTERS, GUILDFORD, SURREY.